Praise fo ‖‖‖‖‖‖‖‖
I0541357

Nikki McCoy

Nikki McCoy brings together a man trying to escape his past and a man who suffered years of abuse at the hands of his lover. The two men work together to create a new life for themselves. The sexual attraction is strong, but trust does not come easily…
~ *Sensual Reads*

A very interesting paranormal story…The many twists and turns the plot takes will keep the reader entertained…
~ *Literary Nymphs Reviews*

An interesting look at paranormal powers…If you like stories that explore a D/s theme in a slightly different way, are interested in paranormal abilities and want to read about a strong alpha male protecting and falling for a physically weaker but very determined man, you may like this book.
~ *Queer Magazine Online*

A great paranormal story…sex is hot and intense…I'd recommend this to those who love light BDSM, paranormal, alien superpowers, sweet protective love and a great story.
~ *MM Good Book Reviews*

Total-E-Bound Publishing books by Nikki McCoy:

Everything That You Are

Keepers of the Gods
Son of Death
Master of Wrath

MY FOREVER

NIKKI McCOY

My Forever
ISBN # 978-0-85715-758-4
©Copyright Nikki McCoy 2011
Cover Art by Lyn Taylor ©Copyright September 2011
Interior text design by Claire Siemaszkiewicz
Total-E-Bound Publishing

Published in 2011 by Total-E-Bound Publishing, Think Tank, Ruston Way, Lincoln, LN6 7FL, United Kingdom.

MY FOREVER

Dedication

For those who have never, and will never, give up their search for forever. Whether it is found in the heart of a loved one, the achievement of a dream, or simply a lifetime of cherished memories, it is there for the taking. We just need to know where to look.

Chapter One

Lucas pulled into the back parking lot of his business and stepped out into the crisp, pre-dawn air. The sky was clear, though the stars remained hidden behind the glow of city lights. Faint puffs left his mouth on each exhale, but it would warm up later. All in all, it looked to be a good day to have his wine-tasting event.

Unlocking the back door, he entered his liquor store, began flipping light switches and adjusted the temperature on the central ventilation system. When he'd opened the shop five years ago, he'd never imagined it would rake in the kinds of profits he made every month. The endeavour was financially unnecessary—he had enough money saved to fund a sizable army—but what had started out as a relief from the boredom of retirement had quickly turned into a wine connoisseur hot spot.

He was proud of his accomplishment. For the first time in his life, he was doing something that didn't revolve around death, although it wasn't always easy. The wine-tasting events he threw every quarter-year were starting to wear on him. As if being here at five o'clock in the morning wasn't bad enough, the paperwork was downright exhausting.

A draught of cold air blew over him and he looked back to see his favourite employee coming in through the rear entrance. "Hey, kid. You ready for today?"

Kyle gave him a wan smile from a face a little too pale for the weather outside. Concerned, Lucas reached out to grab his shoulder as he walked past but Kyle lowered his head and shied away before he could make contact. The behaviour wasn't atypical. Lucas suspected that his aversion to touch was due to some type of past trauma, but during the six months that Kyle had been working for him it had only seemed to worsen.

"You're not looking too hot. Are you coming down with something?"

Kyle adapted a wider, obviously fake smile. "No. I'm fine. Is the shipment here yet?"

Lucas took in the unusually dark bags under the young man's eyes before answering, "Should be here in twenty. The last one is coming about an hour before we open up but it's mostly liquor. We'll have plenty of time to get everything set up before then."

"Cool. I'll get started on inventory then. Save you some brain power for crunching the numbers at the end of the day."

"You're a life-saver."

Kyle continued walking, fishing out his extra set of keys for the office from his jeans pocket. As always, Lucas took a moment to admire the sight of the small man's compact ass through his loose denim. As much as he would like to say he'd hired Kyle based on his credentials, it would be a lie. Kyle had no past employment history. Not even a high-school diploma or GED. But what he lacked in those areas, he more than made up for in customer courtesy and a willingness to work.

Of course, Lucas hadn't discovered those qualities until after he'd taken the man on. He was more than a little ashamed to admit that it had been Kyle's looks and attitude that had initially won him over.

Long, reddish blond hair framed intense green eyes and soft, full lips made for kissing. Kyle was fine-boned, almost delicate, but every once in a while Lucas caught glimpses of lithe muscles stretching and bunching on his arms and beneath his occasional tight T-shirt. The top of Kyle's head maybe came to Lucas' collarbone. And his submissive demeanour…

It called to the Dom in him like a siren's song.

Lucas let out a sigh and adjusted the erection suddenly straining against the front of his pants. Working with Kyle was both a pleasure and bittersweet torture. The man already had a boyfriend, and Kyle had made it clear from the beginning that he was completely devoted to his relationship.

Not that Lucas could have offered him forever. Not with his past. Shaking his head, he proceeded to the back to pull out several collapsible tables and other supplies they would need for the tasting.

Amanda showed up in time to stock the shelves and ready the displays while Lucas and Kyle finished unloading and storing the wares.

"Oh my God. What has she gone and done this time?" Amanda peered through the blinds behind the counter, mouth hanging open in disbelief.

Lucas didn't need to look to see who and what she was referring to. "I told you Mrs Brackney was inviting her club from the Denver area."

"Yeah, but that's a mob out there! And isn't she already a member of the wine club here? Just how many people does she know?"

Lucas chuckled. "Tell you what. Get through the next few days with me and I'll give you both a bonus. I know the hours are going to be rough considering Jay is out of town and Cassy is sick, but it's only for today and tomorrow."

Amanda looked over at him and snorted. "It's not the hours I'm worried about."

Kyle gave one of her dark braids a tug as he walked past to deposit a crate of tequila bottles next to the register. "If any of them try to get frisky with you again, call for me. I'll be stocking the aisles."

"Yeah, right. You get hit on way more than I do."

Lucas grinned at the blush that crept over Kyle's face. It was true. The man had the kind of striking features one simply had to take a moment to admire regardless of sexual orientation. Lucas had no doubt that if Kyle were to switch places with Amanda and run the register, his sales would increase noticeably. He also knew that Kyle would do it if asked, but attention seemed to make him uncomfortable, so Lucas had never pressed the issue.

"But thank you for the offer." Amanda pecked Kyle on the cheek then bounced her plump, curvaceous form to the front door to unlock it, missing Kyle's habitual flinch.

Lucas suppressed the urge to pull the man to the side and ask him again if anything was wrong. He could tell from Kyle's subdued attitude that he was in another one of his funks. While Lucas didn't begrudge anyone their off-days, watching Kyle's lengthening periods of despondency was becoming near unbearable.

"Lucas. Darling! How have you been?"

Lucas found himself enveloped in a flamboyant hug as Mrs Brackney ploughed through her greeting without waiting for a response. "What did I tell you?" She waved her arms theatrically at the crowd bustling in behind her. "This is going to be your most successful wine-tasting function ever. At the mere mention of your name they were marking their calendars. It seems that your reputation for good taste is preceding you. Oh, is that Montrachet? You never cease to amaze me. Collin!"

Mrs Brackney waved to a stodgy-looking gentleman and steered him towards the display of various bottles of wine and champagne placed atop the tables at the other side of the store. Lucas followed them and began the long process of introductions, pouring and placing orders. A crowd of at least thirty had accompanied Mrs Brackney upon opening and more trickled in at a steady flow throughout the day. Lucas tried to keep an eye on Kyle while keeping his ears open to any trouble Amanda might come across while ringing up sales, but by lunch, things grew too hectic for him to divide his attention.

At some point, Kyle relieved Amanda at the register so she could take a lunch break. Lucas inhaled the roast beef sandwich she'd brought back for him in between dealing with customers. At two, the rush began to slow. He took the opportunity to ask Kyle about whether he'd eaten yet, but the young man produced another artificial smile and claimed he'd already eaten. Lucas ground his teeth at the blatant lie. To date, he had yet to see Kyle subsist on more than water and air. He had hoped that the seventeen-hour work day would force the man to consume something, but by six o'clock, it didn't look likely.

Lucas decided to retreat to his office for a short reprieve. He barely had time to kick his heels up onto his desk before a loud crash sounded from the direction of the storeroom. Rushing into the room, he found Kyle on his back with a leaking case of Miller Lite beside him. Lucas shoved aside the box and leant down. The young man's face was lined with pain, eyes clenched tight.

"Shit, are you okay?" Lucas dug his hand under Kyle's back to lift him up but the smaller man rolled out of his reach, a small whimper escaping his lips.

Kyle kept his chest crouched low over legs folded beneath him, breathing rapidly. Lucas glanced around, noticing the small puddles of water spotting the length of the aisle they were in. Kyle had been doing spot clean-ups after the light rain that hit them earlier, but it was next to impossible to keep the floors dry at all times with so much traffic going through. Especially considering the fact that they were short-handed.

"Amanda," Lucas yelled. The brunette came running over and gasped as she took in the sight. "Can you clean this up for me please? I need to make sure Kyle isn't hurt. Mind the water on the floor."

"Of course." Amanda called out to the pair at the register to hold on while she gathered the mop and bucket from the utility room.

"Did you hurt your back?" Lucas laid his hand gently on Kyle's upper back.

"No-o." His voice cracked as he inched away.

"Kyle, if you're hurt, I need to take you to the hospital. It could be serious…"

Kyle cleared his throat and lifted his head, eyes dull with pain. "No. I'm fine. Just slipped."

Amanda came back then and pushed the bucket to the side to pick up the crumpled box of broken glass. As soon as Kyle saw her, he lurched to his feet, nearly toppling over but for Lucas' hand at his elbow.

"I'm sorry. I'll get that."

"Honey, go on and take your break. You don't look like you should be lifting anything right now," Amanda said.

"She's right. Your job won't be in jeopardy if you need to file for workman's comp."

Kyle shook his head with a tight-lipped grimace on his face. "I'm fine. It's my fault anyway. Wasn't watching where I was going."

"Honey…" Amanda continued, but to no avail.

Kyle straightened himself, shaking off Lucas' hold then extending his arms to take the box from her. When she hesitated to relinquish it, there was a pleading note in his voice as he said, "Please. I swear I'm fine. Let me take care of this."

"Kyle…" Lucas growled, but it was too late. Kyle had the box in hand and was walking stiffly towards the backdoor leading to the dumpster. Amanda cast Lucas a confused look but he couldn't give her any answers. The pain on Kyle's face had had nothing to do with his fall, he was sure. Spine or cartilage injuries in the back didn't leave a person able to jump right up and lift weight immediately afterwards. Which meant that his injuries only ran skin deep, and Lucas could see no stray shards of glass on the floor.

"Go take care of your customers. I'll help him clean up here."

"If he wants to go home, I'll stay late with you to get the store ready for tomorrow."

Lucas smiled at the concern on her face, though what he really wanted to do was drag Kyle to his office and find out just what the hell was going on with him.

"I'll tell him, but I think we both know he's a little too damned stubborn for his own good."

Amanda grunted and shook her head. "Just like a man."

They had a mad rush over the last few hours and Lucas had to laugh when Amanda herded the stragglers out five minutes to closing with veiled threats. Once the door was locked and the 'open' sign flipped, she draped her chest over the front counter and groaned.

"I'm going to kill Cassy and Jay for this."

"Go on home. Kyle and I can take it from here."

"Ugh. I swear to goodness, if my kids wake me up early, I'll be changing my number of tax exemptions from four to two. See y'all in the mornin'."

Lucas walked her to her car then locked the back door as he went inside. Forty minutes later, he pronounced the store as clean as it was going to get then asked Kyle to join him in his office. The young man paused while drawing the blinds to the front windows and sent him an anxious look but made no objection. Lucas sat at his desk chair and gestured for Kyle to take the chair across from him.

"If this is about the case of beer, you can take it out of my paycheque," Kyle said in a small voice. "I won't file for workman's comp."

Lucas frowned. "It's about the fall, but I couldn't care less about the beer. Look, I'm not going to fire you or dock your pay. You're my best employee and, quite frankly, I can't afford to lose you, but I am worried."

Kyle tensed, eyes darting around the room in every direction except at him. Lucas recognised it as a fight or flight response, and from all appearances, Kyle was definitely leaning towards flight. Lucas stood and walked around the edge of his desk, hunching down a few feet away to give him his space.

"Kid, I get the feeling that there's more going on with you than you're letting on. Are you having trouble at home?"

Kyle's breathing began to quicken and he tucked his hands between his thighs, but not before Lucas made out the tell-tale trembling in them. A loud honking outside signalled the arrival of Kyle's brother and Lucas laid a staying hand on the man's forearm before he could rise.

"You don't have to talk to me if you don't want to, but my door is always open. I'll help you in any way I can, but I need to know what's going on." Lucas reached up with his other hand and brushed away the lock of hair that was concealing Kyle's bowed face. He watched as a single tear slipped down a pale cheek before Kyle rose abruptly and spun towards the door.

In a rough voice, Kyle spoke, "Thanks," and was gone.

Lucas stayed at his position on the floor, listening to the sounds of Kyle's racing footsteps and the turn of the lock as he exited the building.

Not past trauma. Present.

How could he have missed the signs? All this time, he'd thought that Kyle was dealing with post-traumatic stress. He should have taken into account the fact that the young man lived with his older brother and boyfriend. With two sources of support, a victim should show signs of improvement, not the increasing skittishness Kyle had been exhibiting over the past several months.

Lucas cursed himself for being so blind as he hauled his ass home. Thoughts of Kyle preoccupied his mind, as they did every night after working with the man, throughout his preparations for bed. By the time he finished drying off from his shower and crawling naked onto his bed, his cock was standing at full mast. Knowing he would find no rest until he took care of it, he gripped his member in hand and began stroking himself slowly, from base to tip.

Thinking of the earlier occurrence with Kyle, it somehow seemed wrong now to use the main star in his fantasies to fuel his arousal. He forced his mind away from images of the young man and pulled up memories of the last sub he'd had the pleasure of domming. In the private room of a club, he'd granted the boy's desires to be spanked and caned.

Watching the firm body cuffed to a St Andrew's cross writhe under his steady hand, then sag limply in surrender to the pain and pleasure, had been a powerful aphrodisiac. After taking the boy in hand and jerking him off to a fast and racking release, the sub had been so grateful that he'd wanted to return the favour.

Lucas had allowed him to worship his cock. A moist tongue laved at his balls then slid up his member in long, languorous swipes. Wide lips encircled his head and sucked down until they reached the nest of his pubes. The boy had stayed there for several seconds, angling his head so that the tip rubbed against the back of his throat before sliding up again. Brown eyes filled with gratitude had gazed up at him as his cock was swallowed from hilt to tip over and over again.

Lucas quickened his strokes, using the drops of pre-cum to slick his straining shaft. He recalled gripping the boy's head in his hands and taking control. Small moans had vibrated around his cock, urging his hips forwards each time he pulled that hot mouth onto him. His balls tightened and his member throbbed with every pulse of his heart.

The mental image shifted. When he looked down at the sub again, green eyes stared adoringly upwards through golden strands of hair. Full lips were fastened to his thickness and ignited a fire that boiled his blood. Kyle's beautiful face offered him the power to take complete domination over the scene. And he took it.

Pumping himself furiously, his orgasm ripped through him with an intensity that took his breath away. He came in a profusion of spurting semen, groaning out his pleasure until he'd milked the last of his stores from his still swollen cock. When sense finally returned, he wiped himself off and threw the tissues into the trash beside his bed. That night he fell asleep to haunting dreams of that single tear escaping from Kyle's thick eyelashes.

* * * *

"What are you doing?"

Kyle jumped at the deep voice behind him. He swallowed his heart back down and turned around, making sure to keep his eyes at Craig's feet, which were haloed by the hem of a black robe.

"I'm sorry if I woke you up, Sir. You said I could eat breakfast before I left for work."

Craig approached swiftly and Kyle cringed to the side in anticipation of a strike, but it never came. A thumb caressed his cheek and his boyfriend's malicious chuckle floated down to his ears.

"I did say that, didn't I?"

He remained still, knowing it was a rhetorical question.

"I don't think this job is good for you. You work too many hours."

Kyle felt his breath catch in fear. His job was his only independence. It had taken him years of begging to talk Craig into allowing him to work. If his boyfriend took that away from him, he didn't think he could survive the demands of total confinement again.

"It's just for the wine-tasting, Sir, and only because two of the workers called in. It won't happen again, I promise."

Craig leaned in close, his stale cigarette breath fanning over Kyle's cheek before he took possession of his mouth. Kyle opened himself to the invasion, trying to match the sweeps of his boyfriend's tongue to prove his sincerity, but that wasn't what Craig was after. He swallowed a gasp as the larger man wrapped one hand around his throat while clenching his hip in a bruising grip with the other. Craig backed him roughly against the countertop and ground his hard cock into Kyle's belly.

He was looking for proof of submission, and Kyle played his part as always before things could escalate out of his tenuous control. With a mewling whimper, he forced his muscles to relax and bent beneath Craig's show of dominance. Fortunately, it worked this time. Once the man sensed his prostration, he sucked in Kyle's tongue and bit down hard enough to draw tears, but backed off afterwards.

"Get to work, then. Jake will pick you up at ten tonight."

Craig pinched the tendon just above his elbow and manoeuvred him to the front door. Kyle twisted his head around and took one last, longing look at the eggs he'd been cooking as he was dragged from the room.

"But, Sir...you said I could eat."

The hold on his arm tightened, fingers burrowing mercilessly into muscle until Kyle cried out.

"If you would rather work all day than spend time with me, you have to suffer the consequences."

Gulping back tears of futility, he stopped himself just in time from chewing on his already bleeding tongue. He hadn't been allowed dinner last night since he'd got in so late, and chances were he wouldn't have the luxury of eating tonight.

His brother, Jake, stumbled out after them, still half-asleep, and climbed into the driver's seat while Craig shoved him into the passenger's side. His jaw was encased in a bruising grip as his boyfriend gave him one last, devouring kiss.

"Ten o'clock. Don't forget."

Kyle nodded his head and held his breath, eager to get away from his prison as soon as possible. As Jake pulled out of the long driveway of Craig's mansion, he raked Kyle with his customary, repulsed sneer.

"Gah, you disgust me. Why the hell would you want to work when you have everything you could possibly want here? No wonder Dad threw you out."

Kyle faced the window and did his best to ignore the ensuing string of insults from his brother.

This was not happening. This was not his life.

One day he would wake up and everything would be right in the world again. The way it had been when his mother was alive. He could still hear her lilting, country accent in the songs she used to sing to him at night. Still smell her perfume in the air every time he took fresh linens out of the dryer. Her memory was his one true possession, and he clung to it with everything he had.

Kyle got out of the car the moment it came to a stop behind the store. A gust of frigid wind reminded him that he'd forgotten his coat at home and he rushed to the back entrance. With a quick wave to Lucas once inside, he headed for the cooler and silently begged for his boss to have forgotten about yesterday's fiasco.

His luck, for once, held out.

Amanda joined them shortly, mumbling something about hanging her kids by their toenails if they didn't start behaving. His mood gradually lightened as the day progressed. The shop buzzed with life that helped to keep his mind off the cramps in his stomach for the most part. He declined another one of Amanda's offers of food and was saved from her mounting argument by a customer wanting to know the difference between merlot and cabernet.

If Craig found out that he'd eaten without permission, there would be hell to pay.

Sometime in the late afternoon, when business started slowing, Kyle was putting the last few bottles of Chianti on a shelf when he felt a shove from behind. Beefy arms wrapped around him to stop his forward momentum, allowing him to save the bottle in his hands from crashing into the others.

"Thanks." He turned while taking a step back but the customer wouldn't let go. Kyle recognised him as a member of the wine-tasting club in town. A mop of grey-flecked, brown hair, obviously a toupee, topped his rounded face. His bloated gut pressed into Kyle's flat stomach, despite the foot and a half of distance between their faces. Up until now, the older gentleman had kept his contact with Kyle to furtive glances and the occasional greeting.

"You're welcome. What's your name, gorgeous?"

"Kyle. And I'm taken." He flashed what he knew to be a charming grin to take the sting out of his words. "If there's something you'd like me to help you with, just let me know." He tried again to twist away but the man crowded in closer, moving his hands from Kyle's arms to his hips.

"Actually, there is something you can help me with." The guy took a step forwards and Kyle stumbled back until he hit the shelf behind him. "Are you free tonight?"

"Please don't touch me," Kyle breathed in a rush.

"Come on, sugar. Take a break and meet me out back. I'll make it worth your while."

Kyle turned his head just in time to avoid fat lips making their way to his. He thought about calling out for Lucas when a sharp voice to his left made his blood run cold.

"Kyle!"

The customer immediately released him, but sent one last, leering look his way. "My offer still stands."

The man shuffled away and Kyle looked up into his brother's irritated face. If not for a few similar characteristics, it would have been impossible to believe that they came from the same parents. Jake had everything that Kyle lacked. Defined muscles, charm, height, and an air of confidence bordering on narcissism.

"Outside. Now."

Jake grabbed his wrist and Kyle had just enough time to set the bottle of Chianti on the shelf before he was hauled out of the front door and around to the alley on the side of the building.

"Jake, I..." The stinging slap across his face cut off his defence. Jake bunched the front of his shirt in both hands and slammed him back against the wall.

"What the hell were you doing in there flirting? Do you want to get us kicked out?"

"No. He came up behind me. I don't even know…" Jake reared back and backhanded him, snapping the side of his face along the bricks.

"I have a sweet ride there and I'm not going to let you ruin it because you're a spoilt little brat. You better start behaving or your ass will be right back out there on the streets where Dad threw you," Jake hissed.

"What's going on here?"

Lucas' booming voice cut through the alley and Kyle wanted to sink into the concrete below him. Jake shoved him back one more time before letting go.

"I'll see you tonight," his brother said ominously, then turned and left, wisely giving Lucas a wide berth.

The sounds of traffic filled the sudden silence. Kyle didn't hear Lucas walk away as well so assumed he was still near, but he was too afraid to lift the curtain of his bangs to see. Humiliation at home was one thing, but the knowledge that his boss had been witness to it made his insides shrivel. With a not-too-steady hand, he touched his fingers gingerly to his lower lip and winced when they came away red with blood.

"Let's go inside and get you washed up," Lucas said in a gentler tone.

Kyle didn't want to. He wanted to run and hide from his shame. Even if Lucas didn't fire him, he wasn't sure if he would have the courage to look the man in the eye every day and be reminded of his cowardice. Lucas came closer and clasped one large hand around his forearm, giving Kyle no choice but to walk back into the store with him and down the far aisle to the employee bathroom beside the office. Lucas closed the door after them and guided Kyle to sit on the lid of the toilet seat.

His boss soaked a few paper towels then knelt down to blot them along his lip. "Is your brother your only ride to and from work?"

Kyle felt uneasy under Lucas' scrutiny. His pampering and proximity. Up close, the scent of his cologne seeped into Kyle's lungs, a soothing balm on his frayed nerves. Lucas' face was angled below his, giving him a clear view of perfectly sculpted, thick arched eyebrows above high cheekbones and lips pursed in concentration. Kyle felt the sudden urge to run his hands through the man's short hair. It was as black as a starless, midnight sky and appeared as soft as silk.

This man had at least fifty pounds of solid muscle and a couple of inches on Craig, which was saying a lot considering his boyfriend was a big man. But whereas Craig was built like a tank, Lucas was all sinewy strength and long limbs. His boss had also never raised his hand or voice to Kyle. What would it feel like if hands that large touched him in kindness? Kyle had thought he'd known the gentle feel of a man with Craig so many years ago, but now it seemed more of a fantasy than reality.

Irises as blue as the deep ocean flicked up and peered at him questioningly. "Your brother?"

His brother. The asshole. The asshole that...oh right. Work. "Yeah. I don't have a licence."

"He lives with you, right?"

He could hardly think straight when Lucas centred his entire focus on Kyle's mouth. "My boyfriend lets us stay with him."

Lucas nodded, as if that explained everything, although Kyle still hadn't a clue as to what Lucas was getting at with his line of questioning. Desperation filled Kyle's chest as he reviewed the earlier episode.

"Are you going to fire me?"

His boss stilled, face expressionless. "No, I'm not going to let you go, but I do want you to take my card. You have a cell phone, right?"

Kyle nodded, confused but not willing to push his luck by asking the man why he would hang onto an employee with obvious issues. Lucas pulled a business card from his back pocket and pressed it into Kyle's hand.

"My personal phone number is on the back. Call me if you need anything." He discarded the used towels in the trash then placed both of his hands on Kyle's knees. "Anything, Kyle. Do you understand?"

No, but he nodded anyway, unable to deny the power of the man's gravity. Lucas paused for several seconds, piercing him with those searching blue eyes until Kyle had to look away. He heard his boss sigh and a moment later he was left alone. He wasn't sure what had just happened, but if there was even the slightest chance that he still had a job, he didn't want to give Lucas any more reason to doubt his worth. Straightening his shirt, he left the sanctity of the bathroom and did his best to blend into the background as he finished his duties.

* * * *

Five minutes before closing, Jake laid on the horn of his Mercury Milan in the front parking lot—one of the many luxuries Craig had bestowed upon him throughout the years. Kyle hadn't finished sweeping the floor, but he knew his brother would only come in and cause another scene if he didn't leave right then. He flashed Amanda a bright smile, hoping to dispel the concern written on her face. So far, he'd avoided her attempts to pull him aside and ask him about his busted lip.

Just one more minute, then the day would be over.

He found Lucas in his office, squinting over a document covered with more digits than letters. Kyle rapped on the door, his apology for having to leave so soon on the tip of his tongue, but Lucas cut him off.

"You have my card, right?"

Kyle creased his brow. "Yes."

"Then I'll see you on Monday." Lucas went back to his paperwork without another word.

Kyle couldn't tell whether the man was frustrated at him or the paper. Another long beep told him it was past time to go. As he left the store and climbed into the back of Jake's car, a blonde seated next to his brother twisted around to get a closer look at him.

"Who's this little cutie?"

"No one. Just the kid I get paid to chauffer around every so often," Jake replied.

The blonde gave Jake a curious look but turned back around in her seat. The response didn't bother Kyle. He was used to it. Jake had found out long ago that women didn't exactly fall at his feet once they found out the type of relationship he 'allowed' his younger brother to be in.

Twenty minutes later, Jake parked at the front of the mansion and all three entered with Kyle trailing behind.

The blonde let out the appropriate 'oohs' and 'ahhs' at the impressive expanse of the foyer, requiring Jake to take her arm and steer her towards the pristine sitting room where Craig reclined on a brown, leather armchair beside a lit, stone fireplace. Kyle supposed that once upon a time he had also been awed by the strategically placed, austere decorations and paintings that cost more than his father's yearly income.

The house was designed in a classic, Victorian style with all of the comforts and amenities of modern day civilisation. But now, it resembled nothing more to Kyle than a prison that had long ago sucked away any dreams he might have harboured for his future.

Kyle hurried over and knelt beside Craig's feet with his head bowed, prepared to wait until acknowledged. Jake told the blonde he wouldn't be long and left her standing in the doorway while he walked over to Craig. Bending down so that he could whisper in Craig's ear, Jake calmly reviewed his perception of the scenario involving Kyle and the frisky customer that afternoon. But the truth wasn't enough for his brother. He embellished every line, making it seem as though Kyle and the stranger had been carrying on an affair for quite some time.

Kyle broke his subservience and looked up in horror. The anger on his boyfriend's face grew as the spiteful grin on Jake's lips widened. Yes, his brother had coerced him into a relationship with Craig, and yes, he enforced Craig's rules with anything and everything at his disposal with a little too much relish, but he had never told an outright lie to get Kyle into trouble. By the time Jake was done, Craig was fuming, and Kyle was too stunned to speak up for himself.

Not that it would have mattered.

Jake sent him an evil smirk then sauntered back to the blonde. Kyle didn't have time to react before Craig grabbed a fistful of his hair and threw him to the side. He tumbled across the carpeted floor, coming to rest only when his shoulder hit the hard edge of the ornate, oak coffee table.

Dazedly, he heard the fading voice of the blonde asking, "Should we do something?"

"Oh no," his brother replied offhandedly. "They're into the whole BDSM thing. This is normal. Let's get out of here."

Kyle opened his eyes to see Craig stalking towards him. Fear seized his heart at the promise of punishment on Craig's face. "No, no please," he begged. "It's not true. I didn't..."

Craig kicked him in the ribs twice, stealing his breath. "What's not true? The fact that you were out whoring yourself instead of working a real job?"

Kyle was lifted from the floor by a steel arm around his neck, cutting off his air supply, and dragged to their bedroom on the other side of the house. It was a fairly long distance and by the time Craig tossed him onto the bed, he could do nothing but gasp for breath.

"I gave you my trust." Craig ripped the clothes from him, leaving deep scratches in his haste. "I gave you freedom." Kyle's arms and legs were stretched until he was lying spread-eagle on his belly, tied at the wrists and ankles by thick cords of twine. Craig wrenched his hair back so that he was forced to look the man in the eye. "And this is how you repay me?"

Kyle fought to hold back the sobs threatening to break free while Craig disappeared to the back of the room. "Please, Sir, please. I love you. I would never do that."

The first lash that whipped like fire across his backside cut off the rest of his pleas. He let out a high-pitched scream, but they kept coming. Craig landed a series of strikes from his shoulders to his thighs, each one splitting his skin open so that it felt like he was being flayed alive. Kyle couldn't stop crying out until his hair was pulled back again. Tears obscured the vision of Craig's face but he instantly gave up on sight when a hand repeatedly slapped him over his eyes, mouth and ears.

He could hear distant curses and threats, but his head was ringing too much to make sense of them. The lashes began again and he screamed until his voice gave out. By the time Craig invaded his ass, Kyle had given up his fight for consciousness and slipped into blessed oblivion.

Chapter Two

Lucas dragged himself in to work on Monday with an espresso in one hand and an energy bar in the other. He'd taken most of yesterday off but it hadn't been filled with the relaxation he was hoping for. The images of fear and shame on Kyle's face, along with his busted lip when Lucas had found him talking to his brother, would not leave his mind.

At a young age, he'd been forced to join The Order — an elite group of soldiers among his race chosen for the rare powers they were born with and trained to uphold the laws of his people. So he wasn't exactly keen on the dynamics of family, but he was certain they shouldn't involve abuse among siblings. And where was this boyfriend that Kyle had spoken of? From the young man's behaviour, Lucas would venture to guess it wasn't the first time his brother had hit him.

"Hi, boss! How's it going?"

Lucas squinted at Cassy over the rim of his cup while he headed for his office. Her hair was purple this week and pinned atop her head with a myriad of mismatched barrettes and clips to hold it in place. She was a lot like Kyle. Barely of age to work in a liquor store, but more dedicated and ambitious than most of the older people he had hired over the years.

"Are you sure you can't work evenings?"

"Why? Is something wrong?" She leaned on one elbow and plopped her chin on her open palm, worry creasing her brow.

"Yeah. It's unnatural to be so perky in the morning. It disturbs me."

Cassy just laughed and went back to cleaning the counters.

"Is Kyle here yet?"

"No. He was supposed to show up an hour ago but he hasn't called in. He might have caught the same cold I had."

Possible, but not likely.

Lucas closed his office door and sat at his desk, debating the wisdom of calling Kyle's cell phone to check in on him. Employers did it all the time. Alarm clocks failed. Cars died. Accidents happened. But Lucas wasn't calling merely to see if the kid could work his shift. He couldn't shake the nagging feeling that Kyle was in danger.

After ten minutes of staring blindly at his paperwork, he swivelled his chair around to the filing cabinet and pulled Kyle's employment folder. After flipping open his phone, he dialled Kyle's listed number and got his voicemail after the second ring. Frustrated, he hung up and took note of the time. One hour, then he'd try again.

Twenty minutes later, his cell rang. Lucas felt his chest expand with a sigh of relief when he saw Kyle's number on the screen. "Matthews."

Several seconds passed then a hoarse voice came on. "It's Kyle. I'm quitting my job. I'm s-sorry, but I have to go."

"Kyle, what's —" But the line was dead.

His instincts screamed at him that something was wrong. He jotted down Kyle's address and marched out of his office. "Cassy, can you hold the fort for a while?"

"Yeah sure, but —"

"Be back later." He didn't wait for a response.

Once in his Dodge Avenger, he hit the highway, thankful that the lunch rush hour hadn't hit yet, and took the exit leading to Kyle's neighbourhood. It was on the 'rich' side of town — the street he turned onto full of nothing but mansions and estates. He pulled into the driveway of the address written on Kyle's application, hoping the kid hadn't lied about it. After turning off the engine, he got out, proceeded to the ornate front door and rang the doorbell. A short time later, a man with a slightly smaller build than his answered the door with a sneer on his face.

"Can I help you?"

It wasn't Kyle's brother, and the man looked to be in his late thirties. Too old to be Kyle's boyfriend, by human standards at least, but stranger things had happened. Lucas took in the expensive threads and cropped brown hair over flat, brown eyes. The guy reeked of money without a touch of class.

"Does Kyle Jennings live here?"

"Yes. Who are you?"

"His boss. I need to see him."

31

The man gave him a condescending onceover. "He's indisposed at the moment. Besides, he told me he quit his job this morning."

"That would be the consensus. However, it's imperative that I see him now."

The man narrowed his eyes and started to close the door. "Sorry, but I'm afraid that's quite impossible. Goodbye."

Lucas stepped forwards and placed his boot in the crevice of the doorway before forcing the door back open. "And I'm afraid I'm not going to be that easy to get rid of. Are you his boyfriend?"

"Yes, Kyle is mine. Now if you don't leave immediately, I will call the cops."

Lucas had had enough of the man. "Craig, right?" He shoved past him and walked into the house. Kyle wasn't in sight and from the look of the layout, it could take him too long to search every room for the man. "Kyle!" he shouted. Lucas spun around and ducked the punch Craig threw at him. He grabbed the man's fist and used his forwards momentum to twist it behind his back. "Where is he?"

Craig struggled in his hold, spouting out invectives and threats. Lucas would have laughed if he weren't so concerned about Kyle's welfare. He'd been trained to kill creatures a lot tougher and meaner than the pathetic human in his arms.

"I'm only going to repeat this once. Where is Kyle?"

Craig did as expected and cursed louder. Lucas kicked his feet out from under him and slammed him down to the floor on his chest. He brought one boot down over the back of the man's neck and yanked on the arm he was still holding. With a vicious twist, he bent Craig's wrist until the cords of his neck stood out in hollow relief. The scream that followed was almost high enough to pierce his eardrums.

"In the room! He's in the bedroom!" Craig cried.

"That's better. Now show me where that is." Lucas hefted the man up and grasped his neck in a bruising hold. The house had very few walls, which he supposed was meant to give it an airy appeal, but the furnishings and decorations simply made it feel cold and uninviting. After twenty or so open yards, Craig stopped at a tall door. Lucas opened it and pushed the man inside. Craig stopped at another door which looked to lead to a closet.

Lucas was confused but decided to play along for now. "I'm still waiting to see Kyle."

"It's locked," Craig ground out.

Lucas arched a brow at him and Craig mumbled under his breath as he pulled a gold key from his pocket with his good hand then turned it in the lock. The door swung open and Lucas felt his breath catch at what he saw inside. Craig cried out beside him and Lucas had to forcibly remove his fingers from around the man's neck before he crushed it. He curled his other hand and smashed it square on the bridge of Craig's nose, the crunch of cartilage not even close to satisfying the black fury that suffused him.

"Stay." He threw Craig against the wall then turned back to the huddled form on the floor of the closet. Kyle lay in a foetal position, covered in blood from his face to his calves. From the sour smell of urine, he could tell that the man had been in there for a while. Probably since the last night Kyle had worked. He knelt down and checked for a pulse. It was faint and a little too fast, but it was there.

After taking off his jacket, he draped it over the still body. There was no way he could lift Kyle without hurting him. Most of the wounds appeared to be on his back. As gently as possible, he gathered the smaller man in his arms, letting out a growl when he noticed that Kyle's wrists were cuffed in front of him. Kyle whimpered and fluttered his eyelashes, but his lids were too swollen to open.

"It's all right, kid. I've got you."

"He's mine," Craig hissed. Standing up, he cradled his broken nose in one hand and began to advance on Lucas.

"You ever touch him again and I'll have you begging for death before you die." Lucas meant every word, and from the blanching of Craig's face, he could tell the guy knew it.

"He'll be back."

Lucas didn't contradict him. He couldn't force Kyle to stay away from his boyfriend if he truly wanted to return, but he'd try his damnedest to convince him otherwise. He carried Kyle from the room and house, not trusting his ability to restrain himself from causing Craig permanent damage. At his car, he lowered the back of the passenger seat as far as it would go and laid Kyle down, buckling him in. Lucas then slid in behind the wheel and headed towards the nearest hospital.

Kyle squirmed beside him. "Where am I?" His voice was no more than a soft croak.

"You're with me. Lucas. Try not to talk. We're almost at the hospital."

Kyle shook his head but whimpered again. With the amount of bruises on it, it was probably killing him. "No hospitals. Please."

Lucas drove two more blocks then let out a defeated sigh. He could assess the kid's injuries at his house and if they proved to be more than he could take care of, he would insist upon the hospital. Changing course, he headed to the valley just outside of town. His place rested between two rolling hills, hidden from view of the highway. He'd bought the ten acres surrounding it for privacy, but never imagined needing it to unload a semi-conscious, naked man from his car unseen.

Lucas carried him in and walked through the kitchen to his bedroom on the other side. Pulling down the comforter, he then rolled Kyle onto the black sheets, tugging his jacket from around Kyle's body so that he lay on his stomach. The sun shining through the open windows made visible so much more than Lucas had been able to make out in the dark closet.

The lash marks scoring the length of his body were thin but plentiful. Where they crossed over each other, the skin gaped, showing exposed muscle and even bone in a few spots. Bite marks dotted the backs of his arms and purple and black bruises lined the sides of his ribs. Lucas ran his hands lightly over them to determine if any were broken. When he didn't feel any cracks or protrusions, he pulled Kyle's wrists from beneath him and lifted them above his head, ripping apart the thin, metal cuffs binding them.

In a way, he was glad to see the deep red abrasions underneath. It meant that Kyle had fought against the beating. He would need that strength of spirit to get past this.

"Kyle, I'm going to give you a sedative. I need to clean your wounds and stitch some of them. Are you allergic to anything?"

Kyle shook his head and buried his face into the pillow beneath it.

"Okay, I'll be right back." Lucas went into the kitchen and put the kettle on. He measured out several different herbs, placed them in a tea strainer, then gathered the supplies needed to wash and mend Kyle. Once the tea was ready, he returned to his bedroom and set everything on the nightstand.

"I've got to sit you up so you can drink this." Lucas climbed onto the bed and eased Kyle to his side and then up so that Kyle's back rested against his chest. He picked up the mug and pressed the rim to Kyle's lips.

When he was halfway through, Kyle whispered, "What is this?"

"A recipe native to my people."

"Feels good," he slurred, the sleep-inducing drug mixed in with the medicinal herbs obviously taking effect.

Lucas chuckled and helped him hold the cup to finish off the rest. When the mug was empty, he slipped out from behind and lay the man back down but Kyle clutched the tail of his shirt in one small hand.

"Why?"

Lucas didn't need Kyle to elaborate to know what he was asking, but how could he answer that when he wasn't sure himself? He was far from a Good Samaritan. There was just something about the young man, though, that called to protective instincts he'd never realised he had. When he'd suspected that Kyle was in danger, it hadn't been a matter of whether he should get involved or not. It had been about how fast he could get there and whether or not he should kill Craig.

"I can't lose my best employee."

The herbs started to take effect and Kyle fell asleep with a small smile on his lips.

Lucas awoke to the sounds of stuttering footsteps. He rose from the couch and went into the kitchen, turning the light on as he entered. Kyle stood in the opposite doorway, one hand braced against the dark wood panelling as if to keep from toppling over. His lips were pale and his other hand was held to his stomach, but at least the swelling in his eyes had lessened to the point that he could keep them partially open.

Despite his alarming pallor, Lucas had to admit he still looked damn sexy. A blue cotton T-shirt Lucas had left out for him went down to his knees and contrasted with his ruffled, strawberry-blond hair that fell past his shoulders. After closing the distance between them, he began to guide Kyle back to the room but the smaller man shook his head.

"I feel like I've been laying down forever. Can I sit somewhere?"

It wasn't the best idea considering it might pull some of his stitches, but Lucas found he couldn't deny that soft plea. He helped Kyle to the living room and moved his blankets on the couch aside to clear a spot for him.

"Are you hungry?"

At Kyle's nod, he went back to the kitchen and began rummaging through his fridge and cupboards for sustenance. There wasn't much. He'd have to go shopping soon. He settled on eggs and toast, figuring Kyle's stomach may be feeling a little queasy. When everything was ready, he loaded it onto a tray and placed it on the cushion beside Kyle while he took the other end of the couch. Kyle attacked his food with the fervour of a half-starved man.

"When was the last time you ate?"

He shrugged, saying in between bites, "Friday morning, I think."

"Friday?" It was Tuesday now. Check that—Wednesday, at one o'clock in the morning. Lucas scrubbed his hands over his face, trying to push back the urge to ask a multitude of questions. There was one main topic that they needed to get out of the way before all else.

"Thanks. That was really good."

Lucas smiled down at the empty plate. At least that proved that Kyle's starvation wasn't due to a lack of appetite. He took the tray to the kitchen sink then fished out a bottle of water and a couple of Tylenol. Handing them to Kyle, he sat back down at an angle to face the young man.

"I'll be ready to leave by morning," Kyle mumbled. "And I'll find a way to pay you back." He kept his head bowed, his face hidden behind long bangs.

"Going back to Craig?"

Kyle shot him a look that said 'of course' but only nodded his head.

He bit back a frustrated sigh. "You don't have to go back there, you know. Don't you have any friends that will take you in for a while?"

This time the look was incredulous, followed by a humourless bark of laughter. "No. No friends."

"Kid, he's liable to kill you the next time he loses his temper." Kyle shook his head adamantly and Lucas ground his teeth. "Then stay here with me." A streak of fear passed through emerald green eyes and Lucas quickly clarified his offer. "I only mean to help. You wouldn't be obligated to do anything but work to save money for yourself. Once you've accumulated enough, you could get your own apartment and decide from there whether you want to continue working for me or not."

Kyle shook his head. "It's not that easy."

Lucas rubbed at his temples, predicting a migraine by the time the sun came up. "Hold that thought." Jogging over to the fridge, he pulled out a couple of beers, handing one to Kyle when he returned. "You don't have to talk if you don't want to, but I would like to know why you think Craig is your only option."

Kyle placed the water bottle on the floor then took the beer and popped the lid before taking a deep swig. "I guess an explanation is the least I can give you for your help." He downed the rest of the bottle and stared at it in deep concentration.

Lucas got up and brought the remainder of the six-pack into the living room. "Good. I've got plenty more liquid courage here and no place to go. Lay it on me."

His guest giggled as he accepted another bottle but his face all too soon grew solemn and grave. "My dad kicked me out when I was fifteen — when he found out I was gay. I thought I was old enough to take care of myself, maybe find a job where I could get paid under the table. The kids at the homeless shelter I went to, though... They weren't...they, umm... I just couldn't stay there anymore. After a few months on the streets and a hostage situation, I asked my brother to take me in."

"A hostage situation?"

Kyle sipped at his beer, a troubled expression darkening his features. "I was really hungry and sleeping on a bus-stop bench. Some guy came up and said I could work for him. I thought it was real work. The kind that didn't involve selling myself." Glancing up through fair lashes, Kyle blushed shyly before looking away. "I followed him back to his place. He started doing drugs and tried to make me take them. When I tried to leave, he pulled out a knife and said I was going to whore for him. Seven hours later, his girlfriend came home and managed to sneak me out of the bathroom window. Pretty stupid, huh?"

"No. Not stupid. Everyone is a little naïve at fifteen." What killed him was that he knew he was getting the watered-down version of Kyle's hardships.

"Jake couldn't support me for long. He didn't make enough money and couldn't get laid with me sleeping on the couch. One day he came home with a friend—Craig. His friend said he would let us move in with him if he could have me."

"Have you?"

"As a…boyfriend. I was of age at the time," Kyle said defensively. "And he was nice at first. Took care of me, bought me things. He said I belonged with him." He grew silent, spinning the bottle in his hands. After a few minutes, he continued in a hushed voice. "He told me he was into BDSM. It sounded cool at the time. I mean, who doesn't like a little kink in the bedroom, right?"

The slight tremors in his voice made Lucas want to reach out and encase the smaller man in a protective bubble — place him on a shelf where no one could hurt him again — but he held himself back. If there was any chance of convincing Kyle to stay until he could support himself, Lucas needed to know the whole story.

"I just didn't think it would hurt that much. Or be so all-consuming."

Lucas drew his brows together. "What about your safe word?"

"My what?"

He turned his head away from Kyle, unable to hide the anger he knew was written in every contour of his face. While his previous line of work had never allowed him to have an actual relationship, he'd had his fair share of experiences in domination. He'd even been the submissive a few times to learn his own reactions and detect them in those he dominated. The first and most crucial rule to be adhered to in BDSM was to respect safe words. They drew the fine line between pleasure versus pain and abuse.

When he was able to get his violent emotions under control, he asked, "What did you mean by 'all-consuming'?" Lucas' heart lurched as a tear slid down Kyle's cheek and into the corner of his mouth.

"He started controlling everything I did. Told me when to shower, eat and talk. I wasn't allowed out of the bedroom if he had company over. Getting my job was the first time in years he'd given me permission to be outside of the house without him or Jake."

"And where does your brother fit into all of this?" Lucas growled. At Kyle's startled expression, he said, "I'm sorry. I'm not mad at you. I just… Please go on." Kyle wouldn't meet his eyes, but thankfully his tone was enough to convince the younger man to finish his story.

"Jake was mad the first time he saw Craig hit me, but Craig turned around and bought him a new laptop. After that, the gifts kept coming and Jake agreed to keep an eye on me whenever Craig wasn't at home."

"And that's why you think you can't leave? Because Craig will stop giving your brother a free ride?"

Kyle looked up sharply, a mixture of defiance and pain in his eyes. "Jake was the only one who cared about me when I was homeless. He took me in and sheltered me. I owe him my life."

"And he expects you to pay him back in blood?"

Kyle slammed his half-empty bottle down on the coffee table and stood up so quickly he wobbled. Lucas jumped up after him but when he reached out a hand for support, Kyle jerked away as though singed by his touch.

"Kyle, wait. I didn't mean for it to come out like that. You have to know that what your brother's doing is wrong. He's a grown man capable of taking care of himself."

"I tried to get away once!" Kyle yelled, face now wet with unbridled tears. "He dragged me back. You think he's going to give up his car, his monthly allowance and free rent? They won't let me go." His small frame trembled and he wrapped his arms around his midsection as though to hold himself together. In a ragged, defeated voice, he whispered, "They'll never let me go."

Lucas couldn't hold back any longer. He closed the space between them in one large stride and gathered the slight figure into his arms. There was nothing he could say to that, never having found himself in a position to offer succour to another, so he simply held on as tightly as he dared and made shushing noises. Kyle's shoulders shook with silent sobs and Lucas felt the dampness of his sorrow as it soaked through the front of his shirt.

In a perverse way, he was glad that he'd pushed the man beyond his limit. The feel of Kyle's slender body pressed firmly against his, soft angles enveloped in his much larger frame, was enticing. He felt his cock swell beneath his shorts until it nudged Kyle's abdomen but couldn't bring himself to pull away. This arousal felt different from the lust that had ignited inside him with countless past lovers. It was stronger yet undeniably tender.

After Kyle's sobs diminished to hiccups and halting breaths, Lucas walked backwards, pulling the young man down with him as he sat on the couch. "Let me give you this chance to get away from them completely. You'd be doing me a favour."

Red-rimmed eyes peeked up at him through tousled strands of hair. "I don't understand."

"If I ever found out that Craig or your brother hurt you again, I wouldn't be able to hold back like I did last time."

Kyle's eyes widened in shock then narrowed. "How *did* you get me out of there?"

Lucas grinned evilly. "I have my wicked ways. So, will you stay here?"

The man deliberated for a moment, chewing on his bottom lip. "I can't go back to the store. Craig and Jake will look for me there."

Lucas tucked a stray lock behind one of Kyle's ears. It still smelt of his shampoo from when he'd washed it. Despite the gruesome task of patching Kyle's wounds, he'd taken secret pleasure in making sure every part of him was clean.

"Everything's already taken care of. I gave Jay permission to hire two new employees and asked him to fax me any paperwork for the next few weeks. If there's an emergency, you can come with me so that you're not alone. Meanwhile, you can help me set up orders from here."

"You did all that for me?" Kyle asked in wonder.

It was Lucas' turn to squirm. He could hardly explain the irrational desire he felt to help the man, let alone his attraction to him. "Everyone deserves a helping hand when they need it, and I doubt the store would suffer from my absence for a little while."

"But other than stocking, I only know how to do inventory, and I know you won't have eight hours of papers for me to sort through every day. I won't be able to pull my weight, and—"

"Kyle." Lucas framed his face with both hands, forcing the man to look at him. "If you really want to work, we'll find something, but there's no way I'll let you strain yourself in your condition right now. You *should* be in the hospital. Besides, having you here is by no means an imposition on me." He forced the next words out before he could change his mind. "But if you want me to take you back, I can do that, too."

Kyle sniffed and twisted his hands in his lap. Lucas wasn't sure if the other man's hesitancy was due to him feeling like a burden or truly wanting to return to his boyfriend, but Lucas breathed a sigh of relief when Kyle shook his head.

"I don't want to go back."

"Good." He looped his arms under Kyle's knees and around his back and lifted him easily. Damn, he used to keep dogs that weighed more. His first priority would be to fatten Kyle up. There were muscles underneath that pale skin, but for the kind of work Kyle had done at the store, he must have got by on sheer determination. He just didn't have the mass, or apparently the diet, to have enough energy to heft over fifty-pound cases five days out of the week.

Then again, Lucas supposed one could do almost anything if it meant escaping the hell that had been Kyle's life thus far.

He carried the man back to his bedroom and tucked him under the covers once again. "I'm a light sleeper, so if you need anything else, just call for me." Turning to leave, he was stopped by a surprisingly strong hand on his wrist.

"Please don't go." Deep green eyes glinted in the dim glow of the lamp on the nightstand, shadowed more with fear than by the dark bruises encircling them. Lucas eyed the empty spot on the bed beside Kyle then let his gaze wander down the man's hidden body. He knew what lay beneath the covers—had explored every inch of it during his ministrations. He also knew that keeping his libido in check would be no small feat. It was the shimmer of trust shining through Kyle's desperation, however, that undid him.

Pulling the covers back, he stretched his length between the sheets, leaving several inches of space between them. Without hesitation, Kyle snuggled closer, burying his face in Lucas' neck and curling his hand under his chin. Lucas stiffened as hot breath fanned across his clavicles and warmth permeated his right side through the thin layer of the shirt Kyle was wearing. *My shirt.* For the first time in his life, he was experiencing what he imagined felt like intimacy...and it felt good.

Right.

The vibrations of soft snores tickled his chest less than a minute later and he willed his body to relax. Kyle was scared, that was all, and probably had nightmares. If Lucas could help keep those at bay with mere touch, then he would. The wall of solitude he'd built around his heart since childhood was still intact...and would be long after Kyle found the strength to move on with his life.

Chapter Three

The next several days passed by at a lazy pace. Kyle had never felt more relaxed, more safe – or more confused – in his entire life. Over the course of the six months he'd worked for Lucas, he had gradually grown comfortable with looking people in the eye after being restricted from that act for so many years at Craig's house. In the privacy of Lucas' home, though, he often forgot that he had that freedom with the quiet man. It wasn't that he compared his boss to his former boyfriend. It was rather that living with him felt intimate, in a way. Like a relationship.

He was also having trouble differentiating his desires from his fears. He found that he wanted to do many of the things for Lucas that he had done for Craig. When Lucas had deemed him fit enough to cook, clean and sit at the bed to help with paperwork, Kyle had found himself delighting in the praises the man would bestow upon him. They were few and often delivered in clipped, cool tones, but they made his stomach flutter and encouraged him to improve every time.

Most of them were the same chores he'd done at Craig's house, which had also been done out of a desire to please. He soon realised he'd enjoyed doing these things for years. Maybe not the work itself, but because making another happy made *him* happy. Did that mean it was possible he hadn't tried hard enough to get away from Craig because he'd secretly enjoyed the humiliation and abuse that also came with his former relationship? He hadn't thought that he liked it, and yet he couldn't shake the yearning to please Lucas any way he could, just as he had tried to do for Craig.

He'd seen similar cases on television shows, on those rare occasions when he'd been allowed to watch TV. He had learned to live with pain just as the victims on the shows had. They'd spoken of how, when given the chance to escape it, they preferred to stay. When asked why, they'd said it was because they loved their partner and were too afraid to live without them, but Kyle had always suspected that some of them had grown to crave the abuse.

The thought of his handsome, gentle boss hurting him the way Craig had made him sick to his stomach. He could think of much more pleasurable things for that man to do to him with his large, heavily muscled body. The question persisted, eating away at his mind until he thought he might go mad.

"Hey, kid. Get dressed. We're going out."

Kyle jumped at the deep baritone of Lucas' voice from the doorway of the bedroom. If his boss were a few inches taller, he'd be in jeopardy of hitting his head on the top of the frame. A sleek, black silk shirt moulded to his broad chest, hanging free but not long enough to hide the snug fit of the black jeans that hugged his firm hips and huge thighs.

He had discovered that Lucas had a penchant for the colour black when he wore casual clothes. On anyone else it might have come across as a statement, but on his boss, it made his already mellow charisma feel even more calming. Almost soothing, in a way.

The thrill that always raced through him when he took in the man's sexy features quickly dissipated when that word clicked in his brain.

Kid.

He'd always felt a small amount of irritation whenever Lucas called him that. He was a grown man but he was beginning to wonder if, now that Lucas was aware of his situation, that's how his boss really saw him. After all, how many grown-ups stay in a destructive relationship because they're too weak to get away? Of course, there were the people on those shows, but even Kyle could see that they weren't really mature about their decisions.

"Out?"

Lucas moved into the room with that slow, purposeful gait of his. He began piling the spread of papers Kyle had been working on into one stack, repeating, "Yes. Out. I've been procrastinating on the grocery shopping for too long and you need some clothes."

Kyle looked down at the triple-X large shirt he'd borrowed from Lucas and frowned. Okay, so he had been running around in nothing but the man's T-shirts since arriving here. To his embarrassment, Lucas' drawstring pyjama bottoms had been so long on him, he'd tripped more than walked. But he liked wearing the shirts. They smelt of musk and aftershave, and other than the nights when Kyle could guilt Lucas into sleeping beside him, it was the only constant reminder of the man that made him feel safe — far away from Craig and his brother.

They did need food, however, what with Lucas practically laying down the law that he eat three full meals a day with snacks thrown in here and there.

He worried his bottom lip between his teeth. "You could use my paycheque to get the groceries, and I can give you my size for a pair of pants. I'm not picky."

Lucas paused in his actions and pierced Kyle with his intense, blue gaze. "What's wrong, Kyle?"

"Nothing," he replied a little too quickly. "I just want to get these orders ready for you to fax off. Store's been getting a lot of business and I know it's harder for you to conduct it from here." Kyle broke contact and busied himself with the papers Lucas hadn't grabbed yet, hoping the older man would let it go.

Lucas walked around to the side of the bed and seated himself inches away. He slowly lifted his hand to grip Kyle's chin, forcing it up so that he had no choice but to meet the man's eyes. "I won't let him hurt you again. I'll be with you the whole time."

Kyle started to throw on his façade of bravado and deny the man's accusation of his fear, but quickly realised it was useless. He *was* that 'kid' Lucas so appropriately called him. The one who clung to his only saviour in the middle of the night when the nightmares stripped him of his manhood, reducing him to tears and tremors. The kid who was too afraid to go out into public for fear of seeing his ex around every corner.

He was fooling no one.

In one last vain attempt, he blurted out, "I have no pants to wear. Yours wouldn't fit me, remember?"

His boss chuckled, seeing right through his ruse. "I had Jay bring over a pair of his when he came over yesterday to drop off the spreadsheets, along with some of his old tennis shoes. The jeans will still be big on you, but I have an extra belt I can carve a hole into to keep them up."

"Jay knows I'm here?" A wave of heat flushed Kyle's face and he tried to duck his head but Lucas held him firmly.

"Yes, but not why. That's nobody's business but yours and mine."

Some of the tension eased from his muscles. It seemed as though it would be obvious that the only reason a man as gorgeous as Lucas would have him living in his house was because he was doing Kyle a favour. He was a charity case. And while that may be the truth, it still hurt his pride to know that others were aware of it as well.

"Okay, I'll get ready."

He expected Lucas to pull his hand back and finish organising the papers, so he was completely surprised when the man leant forwards until their lips were barely centimetres apart. Up close, he could see that the blue in Lucas' eyes was flecked with green and grey crystals which sparkled in the afternoon sunlight streaming in through the open window. Kyle smelt coffee and mint on his breath and was held mesmerised when heat whispered over his face as the man exhaled raggedly.

His heart sped until he thought it might burst from his chest as he imagined those hard lips crushing down on his, taking all that he had to give. And then they were on him. Instead of steel and pressure, they grazed along his in the lightest of touches. When Lucas slid his tongue over the seam of his mouth, Kyle's cock twitched and he moaned, leaning in and parting his lips in silent invitation.

Lucas brought his other hand up to cup the back of Kyle's head, holding him still and taking control of the kiss. His senses reeled as his mouth was plundered. He wanted to match Lucas stroke for stroke, to show how much he wanted this, but it felt natural to simply let the other man take possession of him. His body thrummed with excitement.

How many times had he imagined this — bending to the will of one so much stronger than he, yet out of trust and not for fear of reprisal for his inadequacies.

When Lucas gave one last, languorous sweep of his tongue and pulled back, they were both panting. Kyle could see lust burning in Lucas' eyes and wonder hit him anew at the idea that this man, this perfect specimen of masculinity, could find him attractive.

Lucas blinked then shook his head as if to clear cobwebs from it. "I'm sorry. I shouldn't have done that."

Insecurity immediately cooled his passion and Kyle looked away once his chin was free. No, they shouldn't have done that, because he was a kid with a future that looked as promising as a prayer cast into the wind. And Lucas was... Well, Lucas was definitely out of his league.

"It's okay. I'll go with you. Where are the pants Jay brought over?" He tried not to let bitterness sharpen his words, but wasn't sure if he'd succeeded or not. Lucas got up and went to the doorway, retrieving a plastic bag from the floor outside.

"I'll wait for you in the living room."

The large man practically ran from the room and Kyle sighed. Funny how when he'd been living with Craig, all he'd dreamt about was being able to live his life alone, by his own rules. Now that thought stabbed through his chest with a kind of empty finality. He dressed in his borrowed sneakers and jeans, which he had to hold up as he trudged through the kitchen.

Lucas met him at the front door with a flat, black belt in one hand and a pocket knife in the other. He swiftly measured Kyle's waist and dug a hole in the belt to fit. Lucas' movements were smooth and methodical as he looped the belt through the straps around his waist and pulled it tight. Kneeling, his head came to Kyle's abdomen. He bent lower to concentrate on the buckle and Kyle could feel his cock stirring again as he peered down at the bowed head so close to his groin. Fortunately, the pants were too baggy and bunched at the front for them to tent.

He followed Lucas to the car and got into the passenger's seat. The silence between them as Lucas drove into the city wasn't exactly uncomfortable, but neither was it the easy companionship they'd enjoyed over the past several days. As they left behind the sedate, nearly identical rows of suburban houses for the flourishing streets of the clustered shopping districts, Kyle's anxiety began to rise.

They were veering towards the more expensive fashion stores, a few of which he knew Craig frequented when he needed something made to his precise specifications. Lucas pulled into the parking lot of a three-story department store he didn't recognise. He got out and tried to ignore the jittery sensation in his belly, but when he looked out on the crowds of people entering and leaving the building, the enormity of the unexpected turn his life had taken hit him in full force.

In five years, he'd almost never gone out into public unaccompanied or without permission. A queasy feeling settled in the pit of his stomach and he clenched a fist over it in an effort to keep his breakfast down. The last time…

The last time had been when he'd run away. The beating he had received afterwards had been the worst to date, barring the most recent. If Craig caught him now…he wasn't sure if he would survive the man's wrath.

The fear that coiled its way around Kyle's chest and squeezed his insides until he thought he might pass out was nearly debilitating compared to the fear he'd lived with every day in Craig's house. He'd been gone for *six* days, and from what he gathered, Lucas had humiliated Craig on the day of his departure. How much worse would the beating be this time if Craig found him?

His was the fear of the unknown, and he had no way to protect himself from that. He flinched as he felt a hand curl around the back of his neck and pull him into a strong, warm embrace.

"You're safe with me. I swear I won't let anyone harm you and I'll never leave your side."

Lucas' rumbling bass soothed his chaotic nerves and calmed his racing heart. Kyle wanted to stay there, cocooned in the safety of the man's hard body. If only he could. He drew away just enough to meet those royal blue eyes and the confidence in them was enough to dispel his paralysing apprehension. Then Lucas smiled, and his heart fluttered with something that was definitely not fear.

"Are you okay now?"

No. His knees had gone weak and his mouth felt as dry as a desert breeze. "Yes," he whispered. He didn't trust his voice to expand on that. Kyle held his breath as Lucas leant down further. Just a few more inches and those flawless lips would be on his. But they never made it that far. Instead, Lucas pressed them to his forehead then took Kyle's hand and walked him to the entrance of the store.

His boss hadn't been lying. The older man not only stayed close to his side, but retained physical contact at every opportunity. Whenever Kyle let go of his hand to inspect a pair of pants, he received a touch at the small of his back. As soon as his hands were free again, one of them would be grasped in Lucas' larger one before they moved on again.

It didn't take him long to find jeans and a plain shirt within his budget. He placed them into the cart Lucas was steering and couldn't repress a small smile when his hand was once again clasped in a firm grip.

"Okay, I'm ready." Intent upon heading for the registers, he was surprised as he was yanked back. Kyle glanced up in curiosity to meet Lucas' scowl. The security he found in the man's proximity made it easier for him to hold eye contact.

"That's it?"

Kyle followed his gaze to the clothes in the cart. "Umm…yeah. It'll do me for now."

Lucas shook his head then dragged him a few aisles over to the racks of designer wear. His boss looked at the measurements of the pants he'd already picked out and started riffling through those on the racks. He threw at least five more jeans into the cart, followed by the same number of slacks and shorts. Shirts came next. Button-downs, tees, sweaters. On the other side of the men's department, Lucas added socks, boxers, and a few robes to the pile.

By the time they got to the footwear, it was Kyle who wouldn't budge from where his feet were rooted. "Lucas, I can't afford all of this."

Lucas stopped and looked down at him. "This is my treat. I told you any money you earn while living with me can be saved to get you back on your feet."

"You don't understand." Embarrassment washed over him and he glanced at the blurred vision of the mountain of clothes in the cart. He would not cry. He'd done enough of that in front of the man already. Clearing his throat, he said, "Craig took my paycheques. I have no money in the bank. I don't even have a bank account. I can't pay you back for this."

Lucas framed his cheek with one hand and when Kyle was finally able to meet his gaze, he saw only patient regard. "I kind of figured that. As much as I love seeing your sexy ass run around half-naked in my shirts, you're going to eventually need a wardrobe of your own. One outfit won't suffice, no matter how much you enjoy doing laundry. I want to do this for you. If it's a matter of pride, then we'll work something out, but I'm hoping you'll indulge me this once and let it go."

"You think I'm sexy?"

Lucas frowned at him then burst into laughter. "If that's all you got out of what I just said, I'm thinking it's all right for me to pamper you a bit. And yes, I think you're sexy as hell, but I won't take advantage of you. I offered you a safe haven to recover and rebuild, and that's exactly what I'm going to give you. Now, can we finish up here? I'm starving."

Kyle could only nod, dumbfounded. Belatedly, he realised that their whole conversation had taken place in the middle of a crowded department store, but no one seemed to be paying them any mind. Except for the shoe salesman standing a few feet away. He couldn't have been more than a few years older than Kyle, with a wide grin and twinkling eyes lighting his face.

"Is there anything I can help the happy couple with?" The salesman — Mark by the name on his tag — swept Kyle with an appreciative look before giving his full attention to Lucas.

Without skipping a beat, Lucas gave Mark a smile that had the man practically drooling on himself and said, "My partner is looking for a pair of sneakers and also weather-proof boots, if you have them."

Kyle shot his boss a disbelieving look which was met with smug satisfaction. Feeling an uncharacteristic jolt of self-confidence, he decided two could play at that game.

Moulding himself to Lucas' front and throwing his arms wantonly over his neck, he looked up demurely. He thrilled to the feel of Lucas' answering embrace, even if it was part of an act. "I thought you were taking me out tonight, big man. Don't you think that calls for evening shoes as well?"

The man looked surprised for all of two seconds before his charming smile returned in full force. He brought his hands down to the curves of Kyle's waist just above his hips and tugged him closer. Kyle's plan backfired as his breath caught at the evidence of Lucas' arousal. It pushed against his lower belly, demanding attention.

In a voice that sent shivers down his spine, Lucas replied, "Of course. How could I have forgotten?" Without looking at Mark, he continued, "We'll take a pair of dress shoes as well. The most expensive you have."

Before he could protest, Lucas spun him around and propelled him towards the waiting salesman, giving him a light smack on the rump. Mark, as it turned out, was a chatterbox. After Kyle had proved frustratingly indifferent to the styles of shoes he was presented with, Mark began deferring to Lucas' opinion.

When the salesman left to get his size in the chosen styles, Kyle looked at the price tag on the dress shoes and blanched. "You're not really getting these, are you?"

"Would you rather go to the shop down the street with shoes starting out at three times their cost?"

Kyle couldn't tell if Lucas was joking or not, but judging by the serious look on his face, he didn't think so. "That's the last time I flirt with you," he mumbled under his breath. Mark came back and handed three boxes to Lucas.

"Thank you, Mark. You've been a great help."

The salesman looked as though he was going to melt right there at Lucas' feet. Kyle wasn't sure if he felt more disgusted or envious when Lucas gave Mark a smile and the salesman swung out his hip to emphasise his lean waist and long figure. Lucas could probably snap his fingers and have anyone he wanted, male or female. And it's not like they were truly together. It was all just a playful act.

"I work weekends if you ever need anything else," Mark purred.

Disgusted. Definitely disgusted.

"I'll keep that in mind." Lucas dropped the boxes into the cart then manoeuvred it with one hand while wrapping his other around Kyle's waist. Kyle saw the flash of disappointment in the salesman's eyes as he was steered away, and bit his lip to keep from gloating. Craig had never allowed public displays of affection, but then, Kyle couldn't honestly remember a time when he'd wanted to show this much intimacy with his ex-boyfriend in front of others.

The older woman at the register proved his theory correct. She smiled warmly at him but within seconds was completely focused on Lucas. If she saw their hands joined together, she didn't comment or acknowledge it. Once their purchases were paid for, they loaded them into the backseat of the car then headed for the nearest grocery store.

When the car was parked, his boss peered over at him in contemplation. "You're not looking too hot. Why don't you stay in the car while I get the food? You can keep all of the doors locked and take a nap."

His heart skipped a beat at the thought of being alone in a public place without the man's comforting presence. Apparently he hadn't disguised the discomfort of being on his feet for so long well enough, but that pain was nothing compared to the rigid panic that gripped him now.

"Please don't make me stay here. I'm fine, really." Averting his eyes to hide the shame of his pleading tone, he waited with dread for the other man to ridicule him for it. Or worse, make him stay to teach him a lesson in maturity. When a hand came into his field of vision and grasped his leg, his automatic flinch stole the last shred of his dignity. Sooner or later, Lucas would realise he was a lost cause and give up.

"It's okay, kid. You can come if you want to. I was just concerned about your health."

The lack of insults or rebukes gave him the courage to see the truth in his boss' eyes. With a small smile of gratitude, he got out and followed the man into the store. Kyle pushed the cart while Lucas loaded it with more food than he thought would fit in a single fridge and freezer unit. He was more at ease here, knowing that Craig's housekeeper did his grocery shopping—having left Kyle to do the cooking—but he still found he missed Lucas' constant touch.

"Did you want anything specific?"

Shaking himself from his reverie, he looked up at his handsome boss. "Uhh...no. I can cook a meal with just about anything."

"This isn't about what you can cook, Kyle. It's about what you want to eat," Lucas gently admonished. "Don't you have any favourite foods?"

It had been so long since Kyle had been given a choice as to what he wanted to eat that he had to think about it. Normally, he was so grateful to be allowed to eat at all that he didn't care what it was. Memories of his mother drifted into his thoughts. She had always smelt of syrup and spice. Though she'd worked in an office, her passion had been cooking, and she had fostered the same love of cuisine in Kyle when he was younger. He still loved to cook, but the true, carefree joy of it had been lost long ago.

"Pancakes?"

Lucas chuckled. "I've got pancake mix. What else do you like?"

He thought again. "Lit'l Smokies baked in a sugary paste. French toast with powdered sugar. Oh, and mixed fruit coated with orange squeeze." He hadn't realised he was bouncing on the balls of his feet until Lucas laughed and placed a hand on his shoulder, adding pressure to keep him still.

"That all sounds great. Do you remember the ingredients?"

Kyle nodded emphatically. It wouldn't be the same as cooking these dishes with his mom when she was alive but it would be close. The thought gave him more pleasure than anything had in years.

"Good. If you can think of anything else, throw it in the cart."

He knew Lucas had the liquor required to make the paste at his house, so he collected the other ingredients that were needed. It took them longer to pack the car this time, and even more time to unload it once they arrived back at the house. Kyle had begun putting the food away, his mind already wandering to what he would cook for dinner, when Lucas took the cans from his hands and set them on the counter.

"I'll take care of this. Why don't you go get ready for tonight?"

Kyle furrowed his brow. "What are we doing tonight?"

"I'm taking you out to dinner. Or have *you* forgotten?"

He flushed all the way down to his toes. There was a heated look in the man's eyes that told him Lucas was more than up to the challenge of his earlier attempt at flirtation, but he didn't think he could handle any more anxiety. Outside, there were a ·wealth of threats to his newfound freedom, and they all revolved around Craig and his brother. But here, in the privacy of Lucas' home, he could be himself without that ever-present thread of fear he'd come to live with on a daily basis.

Lucas must have sensed his hesitation. He found himself cradled in the steady arms of his boss, taking solace in his solid presence.

"We can go out another night. I don't want to push you. What you've accomplished so far is amazing. I'm very proud of you."

"You are?"

"How could I not be? It takes a lot of courage to leave behind everything you know and make a fresh start."

Kyle didn't think what he'd possessed this past week was courage. If not for Lucas, he would most likely still be in that closet or kneeling at Craig's feet, awaiting his next command or punishment. But he didn't want to argue. Whether it was true or not, Lucas' praise lit a slow-burning fire within him. He couldn't stop himself from wondering what his life would have been like had Lucas been the one to come over that day to his brother's apartment instead of Craig. Would Lucas have helped him? Would he have been as gentle as he was now?

Did it really matter? He was here now, and safe.

Lucas patted him on the bottom and stepped back. "Go put on something comfortable. I'll finish putting the food up."

Kyle wanted to say something—anything—to show the man how much he appreciated his understanding, but words seemed far too inadequate. Instead, he stood on tiptoe and kissed the man's cheek briefly then gathered up his bags of clothing and took them to the bedroom. After emptying them onto the bed, he laughed as he noticed that nearly every article was black.

Chapter Four

Lucas stood in the doorway to the kitchen and admired the slim figure bent over the door of the stove, giving him a perfect view of a tight ass covered in low-riding, relaxed jeans. He massaged his erection for the hundredth time that day while Kyle wasn't looking, trying to prevent the case of blue balls he could feel coming on.

What had started out as innocent comfort at the beginning of their trip to ease the man's worries had quickly escalated to a constant need to hold him, touch him. The power he felt in the trust that Kyle had willingly given to him was more intoxicating than anything he'd previously experienced. Whereas most people had a tendency to grow jaded and cynical under the kind of abuse the young man had endured, Kyle contained a quality of purity that was as stimulating as it was sweet.

Kyle straightened and closed the oven, then began whisking a concoction in a large, ceramic bowl. His narrow hips swayed vigorously from side to side in time with his beats and Lucas groaned. Lust warred with self-loathing and he made a beeline for the living room. He was not such an animal that he would give in to his sexual urges for a pretty face. It was the emotions behind that face that clawed at his rigid control.

No wonder Craig had been so possessive over the younger man. Kyle was not only small and beautiful, but a natural submissive. Lucas had recognised it in him the first time he'd set eyes on the man. Such a combination was sought after by humans and Tsielen alike. It was also often devoured and destroyed like every other precious commodity both species could get their hands on. How Kyle had managed to come away with his spirit intact was beyond him, but he fully intended to keep it that way.

Even if it meant denying himself the pleasures Kyle promised with his sultry eyes and seductive body.

Taking a couple of wine glasses and a bottle of cabernet from his liquor cabinet, he poured them each a drink. He put Schubert in the CD player on low volume then took a seat on the couch while ruminating on how easy it had been to sacrifice his solitude for the little wisp of a man in his kitchen. His experiences in sharing his home with someone had been limited to those occasional times when he'd worn a one-night fling to exhaustion, offering them a spare room to sleep in until morning. With Kyle, though, the peace of solitude had been replaced by pleasant companionship.

Several minutes later, Kyle came out of the kitchen with two steaming plates in his hands. Lucas took one and set it on the coffee table in front of him, glorying in the aroma and presentation of the food on his dish. "This smells wonderful. What it is?"

Kyle sent him a shy smile before taking his own seat a few feet over. "Chicken Cordon Bleu with cornbread stuffing and steamed spinach. Dessert is in the oven."

"Damn, kid. Where the hell did you learn to cook like this?"

Lucas caught the spark of anger that flitted across Kyle's face before he looked away. A few seconds later, Kyle looked back with an expression of fierce determination. Without preamble, the man launched himself at Lucas. Jean-clad legs straddled his waist while the brunt of Kyle's collision pushed Lucas back onto the leather cushions behind him. Kyle wound thin arms around his neck as his plush lips crushed against his. Momentary shock gave way when a wet, seeking tongue brushed along his upper lip, and the offering became more than he could resist.

He grasped the young man's pelvis and ground it against his rock-hard erection, grunting at the jolt of arousal that shot up his spine. Sucking in Kyle's questing tongue, he bit the tip gently before plunging in, seeking out every crevice he could reach inside the hot mouth. It tasted of the sweet aromas that filled the air with a faint touch of pumpkin.

Lucas' cock pulsed and jumped when Kyle threaded his fingers through his short hair and increased the urgency of their kiss. It was then Lucas realised the man was trying to prove a point. He prided himself on being able to spot a submissive or dominant out of a crowd, and this behaviour was far beyond what he deduced came naturally to Kyle.

With a Herculean amount of effort, he pulled Kyle back and saw his suspicions confirmed. That initial spark of anger smouldered in the sea-green depths of the man's eyes, affirming his display of defiance.

Breathing heavily, Lucas rasped, "What brought that on?"

"I'm not a kid," Kyle said sternly, his lowered eyelids belying his sudden bravado. "I haven't been a virgin in years and I can take care of myself."

Lucas' heart constricted as he recalled cleaning the thin lines of dried blood trailing from Kyle's anus to his inner thighs. The idea that Kyle had been subjected to rape, abuse, and who knew what else all to keep his brother happy and stay off the streets brought out his killer instincts, but he tamped them down. Kyle's aggression was born of insecurity, and the last thing the man needed was someone else making the decisions in his life.

Carefully, Lucas grazed a thumb over Kyle's lips. "You're right. You're not a kid. I didn't mean to imply that you can't take care of yourself. I guess when you get to be as old as I am, anyone younger seems like a kid."

Kyle grinned coyly and tilted his head to the side. "You can't be older than thirty."

Add on a few centuries and he was damn close. "Be that as it may, I'm still a dirty old man and if you don't get off of me, I can't be held accountable for my actions."

Green eyes lightened with knowledge and the little imp pressed his crotch forwards before sliding back to the other side of the couch. Lucas clenched his eyes shut and adjusted his aching hard-on, trying to erase the imprint that Kyle's stiff cock had left against his.

"My mom."

"What?" Lucas sat up and rubbed his face to regain some composure, trying to decide if he was strong enough to sit through the meal without taking a cold shower.

"My mom taught me how to cook. Not this, exactly," Kyle gestured with his fork to the food in his lap, "but how to make anything taste good. It's all about instincts, you know?" He took a bite and chewed, face hidden behind a mass of reddish locks. "She told me once that no matter how many times you cook the same dish, it will always be different because it's a reflection of your mood and where you are in life. I think...I think she would have been okay with me being gay."

It wasn't a question, and yet Kyle looked over, silently pleading for confirmation.

Lucas cleared his throat, taken aback by the mixture of wisdom and vulnerability in the young man next to him. "It sounds like your mother was a very smart woman. Did she pass away?"

Kyle returned his gaze to his plate, shovelling another bite into his mouth. His nod was almost imperceptible. Lucas wasn't sure what to say. He'd only known his own mother for the first ten years of his life before he'd been sent away for training. His people didn't place the same values on family structure as humans, but Kyle was hurting and that pained him more than he was willing to admit.

"I'm sure she would have loved you no matter what."

The small man slanted him a brief, appreciative smile that let him know he'd said the right thing. They ate the rest of their meal quietly, the soft sounds of classical music drifting in the air providing a soothing filler. The timer on the oven went off just as Lucas scraped the last morsel from his plate. Kyle gathered the dishes and left to get the dessert, coming back a few minutes later with two saucers and a tub of whipped cream.

Oh, he could so get used to being pampered like this.

Kyle added a dollop of cream to each piece of pumpkin pie, then handed one to Lucas. The first bite melted in his mouth and he groaned as though in the throes of ecstasy. Kyle let out a peal of laughter that was more satisfying than the delicious concoction in his mouth.

"This is amazing. Did you make it from scratch?"

Kyle giggled. "Nah. We'd need real pumpkins for that. I just added in a few extra spices."

Lucas moaned around another bite. "Keep cooking like this and I'll have to give you another raise." The blush in Kyle's cheeks was so adorable, he didn't think twice about reaching out and feathering his thumb along one delicate cheekbone. Blood pooled to his groin and his forgotten arousal bloomed to life when the other man leaned into his touch instead of flinching away.

Kyle's bruises had faded significantly, leaving only small streaks of red and purple along the undersides of his eyes. Lucas longed to erase them—to restore what he was sure had once been an adventurous and confident heart—but Kyle needed more than he could offer. He needed a lover who could devote his life to him...without endangering him.

Reluctantly, he took his hand away and finished his pie. When Kyle moved to clear the dishes, he stopped him with a hand on his wrist and tugged him towards the bedroom. "I'll clean those up. You've had a long enough day as it is. Let's take care of your back so you can get some rest."

Lucas went into the bathroom to retrieve the Bacitracin while Kyle stripped down. This had become their nightly ritual to care for his wounds, but the sight of Kyle's naked body spread out over the comforter was getting harder and harder to resist. Fortunately, only a few more applications of the topical cream would be needed to ensure infection didn't set in.

Lucas took a deep breath and massaged his hard length again, trying to ease the congestion of blood. He settled on the bed beside Kyle and started on his shoulders, smearing the ointment lightly over each laceration.

"Lucas?" Kyle twisted his neck to peer over his shoulder.

Lucas shifted, bringing his knees together to hide the erection straining against the front of his pants. "Yeah?"

"Can I ask you a question?"

"You can ask me anything, ki...Kyle. What's up?"

Kyle's eyes flitted around nervously. After several convulsive swallows, he spoke in a small voice. "I want to please you. But I also wanted to please Craig. Does that mean I'm some kind of sicko and liked everything else about the relationship I had with him?"

He paused, not sure where the young man was going with this. "What do you mean?"

Hooking an elbow under him, Kyle rested his head on his palm. It left his half-mast, slim cock exposed to Lucas' view. Hastily averting his gaze, he sought out Kyle's face and found his eyes locked on the man's moist, parted lips.

"I liked serving Craig. I even liked it when he...when he spanked me sometimes, in the beginning. He said I was a pain slut. That I needed discipline. I wanted to make him happy, but there were so many rules. I felt like I couldn't breathe."

"That doesn't make you sick, Kyle. That makes you a submissive. It sounds like Craig tried to make you his slave."

Kyle lowered his eyes, his long lashes fanning over his cheeks, contrasting with his pale skin. "I want to serve you, though. And I want you to spank me." Beseeching, green eyes met his. "Does that make me a monster for wanting that after what Craig did to me?"

Lucas threw the tube down and gathered Kyle into his arms. "No, sweetness, that doesn't make you a monster. There's nothing wrong with mixing pleasure and pain. Craig took it too far, and he's lucky I didn't kill him for that." He realised his slip when Kyle gasped, but he wouldn't take it back. It was the truth.

Kyle wriggled his body around so that he was laying on his back, staring up at Lucas openly, a combination of adoration and hope on his face. "So it's okay that I want you? Even after what he did to me?"

Lucas gulped audibly. Every reason he'd constructed in his mind over the past week to keep his dick in his pants scattered as Kyle timidly sat up and brushed his soft lips along his. It was no ploy for sex or instant gratification. Lucas knew without a doubt that with a single word of rejection, he could crush the man's frail hold on his self-worth. It added a measure of responsibility he'd never known could exist in a relationship, and one that scared him more than death itself.

But he also knew that he wanted to be the one to grant Kyle his wish. The man craved the kind of assurance only a lover and a friend could give, and damned if Lucas was going to pass that responsibility on to another who might hurt Kyle for his innocence. His decision came easily and with no little amount of joy. Taking the lead, he delved into Kyle's mouth, pressing his slight frame back so that it was pinned between the mattress and his much larger build.

Lucas trailed kisses down the cut of Kyle's smooth jaw, nibbling on the muscles that stretched taut as Kyle arched his neck. He skimmed his hands along the narrow chest beneath him, finding the twin nubs of flesh softer than the tight skin that stretched the length of Kyle's chest. Tweaking both nipples between his forefingers and thumbs, he captured the man's startled gasp with his mouth. Kyle's sweet breath rushed into him in fast pants as he continued his assault.

He pinched the sensitive nipples harder and growled when Kyle's hips jerked up, jarring their cocks together and sending a shock of electricity through his blood. Frustrated by the layer of clothing that separated them, Lucas drew back and divested himself of his shirt and pants. When his engorged cock sprang free, he almost came at the sight of Kyle licking his lips in anticipation.

Moving forwards between Kyle's legs, he nudged them apart then raised them so that they rested atop his thighs. Kyle's cock was thin but long and fully erect, jutting out from a nest of glossy, auburn curls. He took it in a firm grasp and pumped rapidly, teasing several drops of pre-cum from the tip. Kyle bucked and moaned, his hands involuntarily flying to Lucas' grip on him. Lucas grabbed both wrists with his free hand and stretched them high above Kyle's head, denying him access to his throbbing member.

"What do you want, little one?"

Kyle's chest heaved, his eyes feverish with arousal and a trace of uncertainty, but he didn't pull away from Lucas' hold. "I want to please you."

He added more pressure with both hands, leaning on Kyle's wrists while clutching the base of his cock in an unyielding grip. "This isn't about me. Tell me what *you* want."

Kyle shook his head, tears brimming on thick lashes. "I...I..."

I want to please you, his eyes begged.

The ingrained need for this young man to please his lover was written all over his face. Lucas' heart broke even as his cock swelled further at the sight of Kyle's tears. He'd always taken sadistic pleasure in bringing his partners to the point of breaking, but this was different. He wanted to show Kyle that love was not a one-sided affair.

Slowly, he released Kyle's wrists and brought his mouth back down to his slender chest, licking and nipping downwards until the head of the man's pulsing prick touched his cheek. In one swift move, he engulfed Kyle's cock and swallowed it nearly to the root. With a loud cry, Kyle's body arched, involuntarily pushing more of his length to the back of Lucas' throat. Lucas clasped the narrow pelvis and held it down as he sucked tightly on his way up, swiping the tip of his tongue across the weeping slit on the head.

Kyle's whimpers turned to loud cries and gasps as Lucas took him all the way to the hilt again and again, pinching just beneath the head with his lips and occasionally biting with his teeth.

"I'm going to c-come, please!"

"Come for me," Lucas growled. He pumped Kyle's length then took him deep again, working the muscles in the back of his throat around the man's head until hot streams of cum shot into his mouth. Gulping them down and drawing every last drop into him, he felt charged by the sobs that shuddered through Kyle's petite frame. Lucas' body was on fire. He had to possess the lithe creature under him, to dominate him and make him submit.

Lucas reached over to the nightstand and yanked the drawer open so hard it came off one of the tracks. He fumbled for then found the bottle of lube and the condoms he kept in there. After sheathing himself, he squeezed the liquid into his palm then tossed the bottle aside in order to slick his hard cock before using the remaining oil to lubricate Kyle's entrance. Kyle moaned and closed his eyes, causing two tears to stream down his temples. Lucas bent forwards to catch one on the tip of his tongue while pressing a finger into Kyle's puckered hole.

"Damn, you're so tight," he gritted through clenched teeth. He inserted another finger and scissored them, trying to stretch the taut entrance as fast as possible. His cock was ready to burst but he wanted to be inside that delectable ass before he came. Adding a third finger, he twisted them around and knew he'd found Kyle's prostate when the man writhed on the bed, trembling and whimpering in abandon.

"Are you ready for me, baby? I don't think I can hold out much longer."

Glazed eyes opened wide and Kyle nodded his head frantically.

"I don't want to hurt you. Turn over for me." Lucas pulled his fingers away and helped Kyle roll onto his stomach. He lifted the man's pert little ass into the air, growling in approval as Kyle tugged his legs under him, curling into a ball with his behind high in the air. Lining up his cock, he used every ounce of willpower he contained to ease his way in with care. He knew he was big and hadn't fully prepared Kyle to take his girth.

Inch by torturous inch, he slid into Kyle's warm sheath, watching for signs of distress. When half of his length was buried, Kyle charged back, taking him in fully. They both gasped in shock and he gripped Kyle's hips in a fierce hold.

"What are you doing? You'll tear yourself open." Lucas held him still, feeling his cock throb in the channel that threatened to take away his control.

Kyle twisted his head around. "It hurts, but it feels good. Is that okay?"

Lucas wanted to laugh at the man's spunk, but the insecurity on Kyle's face tempered his humour. "It's okay, but you have to let me lead. I don't want to damage you."

An emotion flickered in Kyle's eyes but he ducked his head before Lucas could ascertain what it was. In slow, strong thrusts, he began to pound into the hole that gripped him mercilessly. The soft groans and gasps from Kyle gradually increased in volume and intensity until he thought he might come from them alone. Angling the hips in his grasp so that he pegged Kyle's prostate with each thrust, he strengthened his strokes, hammering into the hot channel, giving it no choice but to accept his invasion.

His balls drew up tight against his body and a tingling sensation raced down his spine, urging him to pound harder. Kyle cried out his name and the muscles in his ass clenched around Lucas' cock, milking his orgasm from him in long, strangling pulls. His explosion burst through him, taking over, and it was all he could do to keep himself grounded by the bruising grip he had on Kyle's thighs.

Lights exploded beneath his clamped lids and what felt like a chunk of his soul was wrenched away, only to be replaced with a searing torrent of emotions so intense, his arms and legs collapsed, leaving him weak and gasping for air.

His loins rocked of their own accord, his cock still spewing its seed and filling the condom buried in the demanding hole that surrounded it. It was too much and not enough all at once. His head reeled with new sensations and his limbs quaked with adrenaline. He could feel his mind begin to fade in a losing battle with consciousness, but a persistent, niggling feeling held him afloat.

Kyle moaned beneath him and he jerked upright, afraid he'd opened the wounds in his negligence. Skimming his hands over the small body, he breathed a sigh of relief when they came away clear of blood.

Something had happened. A vital change had taken place, as though a part of him had been ripped away and replaced with an alien entity. It wasn't painful. In fact, he'd never felt more energised and sexually invigorated, but the implication of it terrified him to the very core of his being.

"Kyle?"

The young man rolled over to his side, stretching lazily, and blinked open eyes filled with bewilderment. Happiness kindled in Lucas' chest and spread throughout his body, flushing his senses. It clashed with his own sudden flare of panic.

Kyle frowned and touched his knee lightly. "Is something wrong?"

That depends entirely on you, Lucas thought.

Emerald eyes widened and Kyle scrambled away, coming to a halt only when his back hit the headboard.

"Kyle, can you hear me?"

Lucas felt the breath expel from his lungs in a rush as Kyle hesitantly nodded his head. Anger swept in and he jumped from the bed, tugging on his short hair painfully in an effort to regain focus. "What the hell did you do?" he snarled.

"N-nothing," Kyle stammered.

Lucas whirled around, taking a threatening step towards the cowering man. "Nothing? You can hear my thoughts, damn it." The joy he'd felt moments ago evaporated in the wake of his anger and distress. "Do you have any idea what you've done?"

Tears welled in Kyle's eyes and he scurried from the bed, nearly falling over his feet as he snatched his pants from the ground then ran from the room. Lucas threw the condom into the trash and yanked on his own pants before giving chase.

"Kyle!" he shouted. He caught the man's arm just as he ran through the front door and pulled him back inside, a little too roughly. Kyle fell against the wall of the foyer and cried out, knees collapsing under him until he was curled into a ball with arms raised over his head in protection. Pain and fear thrummed through Lucas, causing bile to rise in his throat.

Remorse rivalled the unbidden emotions streaming through him. "Baby, I'm sorry. Did I hurt you?" He sat on his haunches and reached for Kyle who flinched and hunched his shoulders further. It was a struggle to disentangle his feelings from that of the frightened man crouching before him and even harder to calm his frenzied nerves. If his suspicions were correct, Kyle could feel his emotions as clearly as he could hear Lucas' thoughts.

After taking several deep breaths, Lucas tried again, brushing back strands of silken hair from Kyle's face. "I shouldn't have yelled at you. I just wasn't expecting you to do what you did. You'll have to give me some time to figure this out." Puffy eyes met his and he wiped the drops that clung to Kyle's lashes.

"What did I do wrong?"

He gathered the shaking man into his lap, berating himself for causing the fear that still coursed through Kyle unchecked. "You did nothing wrong. You couldn't have known that would happen. And I'm just as much at fault. I wanted you so badly but I had no idea you felt the same way."

"What happened? Why can I hear you in my head?" Kyle pressed his palm tentatively to Lucas' chest, over his pounding heart. "I know you're mad. I can feel it."

Lucas squeezed his eyes shut, words escaping him. In one moment of heated passion, their lives had changed forever. Kyle had unwittingly consigned himself to a future of hiding and danger, and Lucas had gained a bond he'd sworn never in his life to have. As long as his emotions were in turmoil, Kyle would pick up on them, and the last thing he wanted was to add additional stress to what was to be an already difficult conversation.

He needed time to adjust to this new development.

"I'm not mad at you. I'll explain everything, I promise, but right now I think you should get some sleep." When Kyle shook his head, he asked, "Do you trust me?" Breath caught in his throat as Kyle looked up at him with a baffled expression. What had passed between them was strong and profound, but it didn't guarantee trust or even love. And as scary as it was, the possibility that the beautiful man in his arms might reject him for it was more than he could bear.

"Yes," he whispered.

The truth he could feel in that answer humbled him. With great care, he tucked Kyle closer and stood, walking back to the bedroom. Laying him gently on the bed, he picked up the discarded tube of Bacitracin and straightened the covers over the lower half of Kyle's body.

"Go to sleep, sweetness. I'll be here when you wake up." By the time he was done applying the cream to the rest of the wounds, Kyle was snoring softly.

Sleep eluded him, however, that night. For hours he stared down at the slim figure beside him, unable to believe what had just transpired. Plans of disappearing again flitted through his mind. It would be so easy this time. He wouldn't have to outrun and outsmart those of his kind, he would merely have to pack up and erase his identity. Hide from a simple human who lacked the skills to track him down. He could leave Kyle with enough money to keep him from want for the rest of his life.

Which could last centuries now that he contained a piece of Lucas' soul.

And what of the threat Craig posed? The part of Lucas that Kyle had taken into himself would not grant the man the physical attributes inherent in Lucas' race, such as strength and speed far beyond the capabilities of any human.

Even if that were the case, Kyle's nature was submissive. By his own words, he'd admitted that he loved to please, and as bad as Craig had been, Lucas knew there were other, more sadistic dominants in the world that would jump at the chance to take advantage of one so naïve and appealing.

On the other hand, staying in Kyle's life would mean introducing him to risks deadlier than Kyle could imagine. Lucas' past would always haunt him, and he had no right to force another to live with his regrets.

As the morning sun crested the eastern hill and cast its rays through the window pane in the far wall, Lucas watched the soft glow light up the delicate features of Kyle's face. This man had chosen him. The realisation was daunting and exhilarating at the same time. It was a poor choice and made in ignorance, but he was fully aware of the requirements for a true bonding, for all he had tried to avoid it.

This sexy, kind, giving little wisp of a man had sacrificed a piece of his soul, capturing a part of Lucas' in return. Was he seriously thinking of spurning what could be the best thing that had ever happened to him?

And to think he prided himself on his intellect.

A wide grin split his face and he bit his cheek to keep from laughing aloud. Kyle was his. Accepting that fact was like finding solid ground in a whirlwind of doubt. Now all he had to do was convince Kyle of this.

Propelled by his new-found resolution, he placed a feather-light kiss on his lover's forehead then dressed to make breakfast. Pancakes. He recalled Kyle showing an interest in them. Whipping up the batter in a bowl, he poured a few handfuls of blueberries in then set about making several stacks. The first batch came out burnt, his cooking skills more rusty than he'd thought, but by the time he was done, a golden mountain of pancakes overflowed the plate on the counter.

A shuffling noise behind him drew his attention and he turned to see Kyle standing nervously in the doorway. "Shit, I was hoping to be there when you woke up." Lucas put down the spatula and went to pull him into a careful hug. "How are you feeling?"

"Weird. And you feel…happy. How do I know that?"

"Let's talk after we eat." He tugged Kyle towards the chair with a pillow on it and sat him down. "I know these aren't as great as you would have made them. It's been a while since I cooked something that took more than five minutes in the microwave to prepare."

Kyle flashed him a small smile while he piled enough pancakes to feed three onto a separate plate. His own method of encouraging the man to eat as much as possible.

After several minutes, Kyle looked up and gave a strained giggle. "Okay, you're freaking me out. Did I grow horns or something?"

"What?"

Kyle slanted his gaze to the loaded fork forgotten in Lucas' raised hand. "You've been staring at me since I came in. It's about what we did last night, isn't it?"

Lucas sighed. He'd taken so long to come to terms with their situation that he had yet to formulate the right words to break the news to him. "In a way, it does. Finish eating, though. This conversation could take a while."

Kyle shovelled one more bite into his mouth, then muffled out, "I'm done."

Lucas narrowed his eyes at the little imp but held his tongue. He couldn't blame Kyle for his impatience any more than he could keep stalling the inevitable. He packed the leftovers into a container and gathered his thoughts as best he could while Kyle cleared the dishes from the table.

Once they'd moved to the living room, he gestured for the man to sit on the couch while he paced the floor in front of it.

Subtlety had never been one of his strong points so he decided to go for blunt honesty.

"I am Tsielen. A race that came to your planet several hundred years ago. I won't go into all of the gory details of why several of us chose to move here, but suffice it to say, we've built a fairly strong establishment. My kind is very different from yours, but for the most part we've managed to coexist peacefully. That's largely due to the fact that we keep our existence hidden from humans, though there are some who know of us. We possess abilities superior to your race and some that are...different." He stopped to look at Kyle, trying to gauge his feelings, but there was nothing.

Kyle continued to stare at him with a blank expression, which Lucas found increasingly unnerving with each second that passed.

"Show me," he said finally.

"Show you what?"

"One of your abilities."

Lucas frowned, not sure what to make of Kyle's reserved attitude. Using his power was out of the question, which left him with the options of displaying his speed or strength. Glancing around, he plucked a cast iron poker from its holder and grasped both ends. Applying a small amount of force, he broke it in half with a loud snap, holding the two halves up for Kyle's inspection.

The man's jaw dropped in shock. Rising from the couch, he kept his eyes fixated on the rod and hesitantly touched one jagged tip with a finger. "Does this have to do with why I can hear you in my head?"

"Yes and no."

Kyle scowled up at him. "What kind of an answer is that?"

Chuckling, he replied, "Patience, sweetness. Maybe you should sit back down." Tossing aside the ruined poker, he guided Kyle to the couch and took a seat next to him. "Do you remember making love last night?"

Kyle's face flamed bright red and he ducked his head. "Yeah."

Damn, the man was cute when he blushed. "You...*we*...bonded. We exchanged parts of our souls and, in doing so, created a connection that cannot be undone."

"Because we had sex?"

"Made love," Lucas corrected. "And it takes more than that act for my kind to bond. You gave yourself to me completely...and I guess I did the same. Without any reservations, pieces of our souls were transferred and infused. You can now feel my emotions and hear my thoughts when I broadcast them, just as I can yours."

The young man shook his head. "What are you saying?"

"I'm saying that you became my soul mate." It felt so right to acknowledge it. Kyle belonged to him now, no matter what the consequences.

The man laughed with a touch of hysteria then sobered just as quickly. "Wait. This is why you were mad last night, isn't it? Because we supposedly bonded?"

Lucas nodded slowly, unable to keep it a secret. Kyle was as strongly attuned to his emotions as he was to those of his mate.

"So this is my fault. I somehow tied you to me when you never really wanted me in the first place."

"Kyle, that's not what I'm saying. It takes two to create a soul bond..."

Kyle shook his head furiously, refusing to listen to anything else. "I won't be your addiction," he said softly. "I c-can't. Not again." Kyle leapt from the couch and ran to the front door. Lucas used his enhanced speed to cut him off, unabashed at exposing his preternatural abilities in front of the man now that they were mated. With a startled cry, Kyle skidded to a halt then spun around, tripping over the foyer table in his haste.

Lucas snatched him up, preventing his fall, and held him tight as Kyle struggled in his hold. Feelings of fury and terror ripped through him with such ferocity that it took all he had to keep his own emotions from reverberating. Despite the severity of his mate's panic, he became aware of dampness on the front of his shirt and cursed. Kyle was tearing himself apart in his effort to escape.

Suddenly, his mate went limp in his arms and desolation replaced resistance. Lucas nearly drowned in the sorrow that radiated from the little man. It was as though all of the pain and degradation Kyle had been forced to endure in his life had come to be too much, stripping him of his strength and spirit.

"Kyle, sweetness, please stop this. I need you to talk to me." When there was no response, he picked him up and took him back to the couch. They still had a lot to discuss, but Kyle's safety came first. "You tore open some of the cuts on your back. Will you stay here while I get a cloth and medicine?" Again there was no reply. He would have to trust the emotions he felt from his mate to warn him if Kyle tried to take off a second time.

Planting a chaste kiss on his forehead, Lucas then went to the kitchen and created the same concoction he had upon Kyle's arrival to help with the pain, only without the herb that would put him to sleep. The stitches needed to come out, but he suspected a few would have to be replaced. After gathering the supplies from the bathroom, he let out a breath of relief when he found Kyle sitting where he'd left him.

He placed the bowl of warm water and rubbing alcohol on the floor, then carefully peeled Kyle's shirt off. Lucas helped him to drink the tea then asked him to lie down. Stitches on the deepest lacerations had torn through the skin but thankfully the wounds hadn't reopened completely.

Lucas knelt down and washed the blood away in soft strokes then set tweezers and scissors into the rubbing alcohol to sterilise. Staring down at the quiet man, he never would have imagined Kyle capable of tolerating and hiding such turbulent emotions. On the outside, his face remained impassive, his body pliant, but inside a storm raged the likes of which not even Lucas, with his violent past, could compete with.

"Is that what you were to Craig? An addiction?"

A pang of misery flared but was quickly tamped down. Silence governed the room for so long that Lucas gave up hope for an answer. Which he could live with...for now. What really caused his own fear to intensify was the gradual lessening of Kyle's emotions. The churning riot of distress dimmed with each passing minute until his mate seemed as detached on the inside as he was out.

"*I won't push you*," he thought, trying to salvage a measure of the intimacy they had shared last night. "*I know this is a lot to take in, and my reaction only made it worse.*" Lucas took the tweezers and scissors from the bowl and laid a kiss on the edge of one laceration before removing the stitches from that area to give Kyle warning. "*The truth is, I've done a lot of things in my past that I'm not proud of.*" He kissed along a second slash and removed the stitches from there.

"*I've led a very dangerous life, and for that reason I never wanted to fall in love.*" Another kiss and a few more stitches.

"But you changed that. I don't think our perceptions of addiction are the same, but I have been addicted to you ever since I first saw you. Your determination, your spirit."

Pausing to gather his thoughts, he took out the last of the stitches and threaded a needle to repair the damage done earlier. *"I don't regret what happened. I would change it if I could, but there's no turning back from this."*

Kyle twisted around to slant him a sceptical look. "Wow. You really suck at romance."

Barely managing to keep his hand aligned with the thread he was about to tie off, Lucas gaped at the sarcasm in his mate's tone. If not for the sliver of humour that sparked from Kyle and twined its way into Lucas' heart, he would have been seriously offended. Maybe. The man did have a point. He knew nothing about love and relationships.

"Okay, so I have no skills, but at least I got a reaction out of you. Does this mean you're talking to me again?"

His mate buried his face in his arms, the curtain of his hair hiding him from Lucas. Centuries of being a killer, of learning to control his emotions and dissociate himself from the demands of his job, could never have prepared him for this. Kyle needed space, which was the one thing Lucas should have been able to excel at, but now found next to impossible.

Everything in him wanted to reach out and reassure Kyle that this new development was a good thing—that they could both be happy if they accepted it. But how could he when his own doubts prevented him from doing that? By rescuing Kyle, he'd inadvertently put the man in more danger. He finished up the last stitch, rubbed the antibacterial cream over the opened wounds then set everything aside.

"Can I have some time to think about this?" Kyle muffled, keeping his face concealed.

"Of course. I'll, um...I'll be in my study if you need anything." He collected the supplies and gave his mate privacy, willing himself with all that he had not to turn around and disregard Kyle's request.

Chapter Five

The anxiety had been building in his chest for the past twenty minutes, letting him know it would come soon. Kyle halted his writing and held his breath. Like clockwork, the faint caress of Lucas' deep voice sounded in his head.

"Kyle?"

He smiled secretly and released his breath, trying to dispel the butterflies that swirled in his stomach. *"In the bedroom doing paperwork,"* he replied.

The anxiety instantly eased, as Kyle knew it would, and with it he felt his own angst fade. It had been unnerving at first, the way their emotions not only infused one another, but also played in tandem. The moment Lucas began to feel a strong emotion, such as stress, Kyle's body would involuntarily react, and vice versa, he suspected. It gave new meaning to the word 'empathy'. Thankfully, weaker emotions could only be felt as a low humming sensation in the background.

It had also been extremely annoying, and frightening, to put up with Lucas constantly contacting him through their mental link simply to check up on him. It reminded him of the kind of possessiveness Craig had been quick to reveal and take pride in, but there was a difference that Kyle wasn't sure how to deal with, though impossible to ignore.

After the fifth brief enquiry by Lucas, Kyle had not bothered to hide his irritation and the answering flare of abashment from Lucas has taken his breath away. Even though it had faded almost immediately, it'd been just enough to make him realise he wasn't the only one affected by this...connection they had. Since then, he'd noticed a subtle hesitancy behind the anxiety when Lucas contacted him every other hour, which made all the difference between the relationship he'd known with Craig and what he was discovering now.

"We have company, sweetness. Would you like to come out here?" A flare of panic surfaced and Lucas amended, *"It's only Amanda. She wants to say hi to you."*

Relaxing a bit, he jumped up and ran to the bathroom to inspect his reflection. The last of the stitches had come out this morning, allowing him a little more freedom of movement, and the discolouration of the bruises had finally disappeared. His appetite had waned since he'd learnt about Lucas' secret and found himself in an undesired bonding, but then again, the habitual dark circles under his eyes were fading.

He'd slept better over the past few nights than he ever had in his life. Though Lucas kept his promise of distance during the day, Kyle still needed his presence at night to keep the nightmares at bay, but it was so much better now. Even in sleep, he could feel the man's strong, soothing comfort. Whispers of contentedness would enfold him in a sheltering embrace that kept him in a peaceful state from the moment he closed his eyes until the morning sun woke him.

Stacking the papers onto the dresser and slipping on a pair of socks, he padded out to the living room where he saw Amanda leaning close to Lucas, whispering quietly. A sense of foreboding went through him as he took in the grim expression on Lucas' face. The moment Amanda caught sight of him, though, she smiled widely and rushed over to squeeze him in a tight hug. Lucas darkened and took a step forwards.

"It's okay. I'm fine."

The big man hesitated but backed off. Kyle decided the pain of her embrace was definitely worth the knowledge that Lucas wanted to protect him, even from friends. Amanda stood back and looked him over, touching his face and hair as a mother would a child who had been away for too long.

"Oh, you're looking so much better. Have you gained weight? And there's actually colour in your cheeks! My, my, my, what have you two been doing up here away from everyone?" At Kyle's deep flush, she laughed and gave him another hug. "I'm just kidding. I had to bring over more spreadsheets and thought I'd see what you were up to." She glanced at Lucas who apparently took that as a cue.

"I need to go out back and check on my firewood supply. There's supposed to be a cold front coming in soon." After setting the stack of papers in his hand onto a side table, he walked to the sliding glass doors that led outside. "Call if you two need anything." With that, he was gone. Kyle frowned at Amanda but she paid it no mind, leading him to the couch to sit next to her.

"So how have you really been doing? You don't have to tell me anything specific, I'm just worried about you. Jay told me you were here but not why."

He smiled at her roundabout way of getting information. For all her nosiness, she truly did care about others and never pushed a person's boundaries. Admittedly, she did gossip, but only to her husband who was about as grumpy and antisocial as any old man could get.

"I'm doing good. Lucas is helping me through some...problems."

"Oh honey," she said, her look of sympathy matching the consoling touch of her hand on his cheek. "I'm so proud of you. Everyone needs a little help at some point in their lives, and I'm sure this is what you need right now. You look so much happier than before."

It was easy to be around Amanda. She was a no-nonsense woman of the earth—a lot like his mother had been—but he couldn't talk about his reasons for being here. Not yet at least. She seemed to sense that and let the subject drop.

Her face grew serious and Kyle's foreboding returned. "There's another reason why I came here. Your brother stopped by the store yesterday asking about you." And the topic went from bad to worse. "Demanding, actually. He came in raising all kinds of hell. I told him that you quit a week ago and I haven't seen you since, but he wouldn't take no for an answer. I had to resort to threatening him with calling the cops if he didn't leave."

The slight tremor in his hands spread throughout his body like wildfire. He'd known Craig and Jake would search for him, but the confirmation of it terrified him

Nikki McCoy

more than he'd expected. Despite the stress of his newfound connection with Lucas, staying here with the man had lulled him into a false sense of security.

He'd been deluding himself. They would find him. It was only a matter of time before Craig figured out that he was living with his boss, if he hadn't already. He barely registered the slamming of the door before Lucas was kneeling at his feet, taking his shaking body into his arms and rocking back and forth.

"They will not get you. I won't allow it!"

Amazingly, the vehemence in Lucas' mental voice calmed him a degree. Wetness smeared his face as he slid it along the fabric of the man's shirt and burrowed deeper, ashamed of the tears he hadn't known were there.

"You are mine, and I will kill anyone who tries to hurt you again. Do you hear me?"

He shuddered once then melted into the solidity of Lucas' body and emotions. They were fierce and rife with savage certainty, but they also gave him strength. When he eventually pulled back, Lucas was reluctant to let go, which brought an unexpected grin to his lips. His feral, protective hero.

"I'm good now. It just took me by surprise."

Lucas framed his head with both hands and stared into his eyes. Using both thumbs, he brushed away the tracks of Kyle's tears then leaned in to press their lips together lightly. "Never again. I won't let it happen. Not for as long as you live."

In a quavering voice, Kyle asked, "You'll find me no matter what, huh?"

Lucas grinned. "I have my wicked ways, remember?"

Laughter bubbled up in Kyle's chest and he let it out, grateful for the relief of tension. "Really, I'm all right."

When Lucas refused to budge, he switched tactics. "Steak dinners in front of a cosy fire?" The man seemed to finally take the hint and left them alone again. When Kyle thought he was ready to bear the disapproval in Amanda's eyes, he looked up at her, but there was no censure there.

The robust woman merely smiled with a contemplative expression. "I had a friend once who was being abused by her husband. For years she hid it from everyone. Told me she had occasional bouts of depression and wouldn't leave the house for days because of it. One day, I went to visit her and she was gone. She and her husband had moved without a forwarding address or notice to their landlord.

"It wasn't until I talked to her neighbours that I found out about the abuse. By the time they were done telling me of the numerous times they'd felt compelled to call the cops for fear her life was in danger, I felt like the worst friend in the world. How could I not have seen the signs? She was such a sweet little thing when I met her. Atrociously happy all the time."

Her eyes welled with tears but she blinked them back. "I've been searching for her for more than two years now. Granted, it's partly because of my guilt. Never once did I suspect... Well, it makes me wonder what might have happened if someone had offered her a permanent way out. My husband is forever reminding me that abuse happens all the time, but for that one person that it's happening to, there's nothing common about it. And there shouldn't be."

Kyle fidgeted, wringing his hands together, not sure how to respond.

"Do you know I have never seen or heard of that man having a significant other, or even going out a date, since

I've known him?" Following her gaze to the glass doors, he saw the bare-chested form of Lucas hefting an axe high above his head and bringing it down in a graceful arc. "Not in the four years I've been working for him." She snorted. "Come to think of it, he hardly socialised with any of his employees until you came along. Guess that makes you special indeed, doesn't it?"

Flushing at her innuendo, he said, "We're not dating. He's only…"

"Helping you through some problems," she threw back at him. "Well, whatever his reasons, I'm glad for the both of you. Just remember, people show their loneliness in different ways. Some clam up, others go about their lives as though nothing is wrong until someone comes along and turns their perfectly ordered world upside down."

She glanced out the window again, compassion glowing in her eyes. "Anyway," she said, patting him on the leg, "I have to go unglue my kids from their X-Box so they can do their chores. I swear, whoever invented those things should be dragged out into the street and shot. And don't worry about your brother, dear. Lucas gave me permission to call the cops immediately if he ever sets foot on store property again."

She stood, then leaned over to place a hand on his cheek. "You're a sweetie. I don't blame Lucas in the slightest. Tell him I said 'bye, will you?"

He frowned at her cryptic words but nodded. "Sure, Amanda. Thanks for the warning." He walked her to the front door then returned to the couch to mull over their conversation. Lucas' lean, heavily muscled build drew his gaze outside and he began to wonder what other secrets lay behind the man's normally cool façade.

He would never have suspected his boss of being insecure, and yet he felt it every time Lucas checked in on him. Then there was the secret of his race and abilities. Lucas had also divulged that it took both partners to create the kind of bond they had, which meant that he must have cared for Kyle as much as Kyle had him during their brief moment of passion. Or had it been all along like Amanda suggested? Several people had witnessed Craig hurting him, yet none of them had raised their voice in opposition, let alone taken action against it as Lucas had.

The idea that such a large, confident man was lonely struck him as a little unbelievable, but then, he'd gone for years without anyone suspecting the same of him. Suddenly, his reasons for shutting Lucas out seemed selfish. Amanda was absolutely right about one thing. Lucas had turned his life upside down to help him while asking for nothing in return. The least Kyle owed him was an explanation for his reticence towards him.

Kyle slipped on his sneakers, went out back and slowly approached Lucas. Long, sleek lines covered in a light sheen of sweat gleamed in the sunlight. Form-fitting jeans rode just below his tapered waist and hugged his rounded ass nicely. There was a stylised, circular tattoo between his shoulder blades that drew attention to the sinuous muscles that flexed and bunched along his back.

Pausing to admire the sight, Kyle felt his heart skip at the realisation that this gorgeous man wanted him. Maybe not for a relationship, but the fact of their bond had to count for something.

Lucas turned then, as though sensing him, and Kyle's eyes roamed as if of their own accord over the planes and angles of his body. Scars he hadn't noticed before stood out in pale contrast to his tanned flesh. They were faded and appeared to have been made by weapons, which only added to his rugged appeal.

Kyle's mouth went dry and blood pooled to his groin, pushing his engorged cock painfully against the teeth of his zipper. When his eyes rose to meet Lucas', the lust he saw in them fuelled his own, burning him with its intensity. What gave him the courage to act on his arousal, however, was the hesitancy he felt in the man's emotions.

Lucas would never hurt or rush him. He knew it then without a single doubt in his mind or heart. Memories of Craig's cruel abuse vanished in the face of that knowledge. Kyle nodded, giving Lucas the permission he was waiting for.

The axe hit the ground and Lucas strode forwards. Kyle shivered, expecting the man to be rough in his eagerness, but he was met with the softest kiss, like the brush of wings along his lips, and hands that threaded tenderly through his hair. The uncertainty was still there and Kyle wanted nothing more than to remove it — to show the man that he was ready. Taking the initiative, he deepened the kiss, melding their bodies together so that his cock rubbed along a thick thigh.

Growling, Lucas circled his arms around Kyle and bent him backwards, taking control and ravaging his mouth with abandon. It was so easy to let go completely. Lucas' presence permeated his entire being, filling his senses and devouring him until nothing else existed but the heat and desire that flamed between them.

When they finally broke apart, both were breathing heavily. "Are you sure?"

"Yes. Yes, I'm sure. Now shut up and kiss me again."

Lucas chuckled and gave him what he wanted. Kyle was lifted by his ass and instinctively wrapped his legs around the man's waist without breaking their kiss. So absorbed was he in the feel of the powerful body holding him that he didn't recognise their changing surroundings until Lucas laid him down on the bed. When he sat up and tried to pursue the man's retreating form, a firm hand pushed him back down.

"Get undressed for me. I'm not going anywhere."

Kyle scrambled to get his clothes off, watching Lucas' movements with rapt attention. Lucas stripped down quickly then walked over to his dresser. From the top drawer, he pulled out several items and placed them on the side of the bed. Once Kyle could see each piece clearly, panic shot through him and he glanced questioningly at the large man.

"I know that you desire pain and fear it at the same time. I want to show you that you have nothing to be ashamed or afraid of here. Do you trust me to do that?"

His gaze travelled back to the instruments. They were essentially harmless compared to the ones Craig had used to inflict serious pain. He gave himself a mental shake to banish thoughts of his former boyfriend from his mind. The bastard had stolen five years of his life. Allowing Craig to influence his recaptured freedom only put him in a different kind of prison. One with no walls and still no hope.

"I trust you," he said, looking up in time to see an approving smile.

Lucas picked up two pairs of black, leather cuffs and guided Kyle to lie on his back in the middle of the bed. He snapped one cuff of each pair to the bars on either side of the headboard then began stretching Kyle's arms to attach the other ends of the cuffs to his wrists. Kyle's breathing came rapidly and sweat dampened his brow.

"Shhh, baby. Try to relax your muscles and concentrate on what I'm feeling. I'm right here with you."

A wave of warmth and excitement rushed into him at that same moment Lucas possessed his mouth, drawing a moan from him. Sure hands explored every inch of his chest and sides, squeezing in some places and feathering over others. By the time Lucas ran his tongue down the curve of his neck and sucked one nipple into his hot mouth, the cuffs were all but forgotten.

Lucas alternated between biting and sucking, then moved on to the other nipple. The combination had his cock begging for attention but he knew he couldn't ask for it. He wanted to experience true submission and trusted this man to know what he needed. Lucas sat up and reached over for the pair of nipple clamps.

"For now, we'll use 'stop' as your safe word. Even though I can sense your emotions, verbal communication is important. At any time you feel overwhelmed, I want you to say 'stop', is that clear?"

Kyle nodded but kept his eyes trained on the clamps.

"Look at me, sweetness. Focus only on me."

It was difficult to tear his gaze from the devices, but once those blue eyes caught his, he was held transfixed. Lucas pinched one nipple then latched a clamp to it. Kyle sucked in a breath and held it as the man repeated the process on the other side. His breath was swallowed in an even more commanding kiss than the last until the pain ebbed.

Lucas then took the last of the items from the edge of the bed and used a lighter to light the small, white candle. This was something new to Kyle, though he'd heard of it before. Setting the candle in a holder on the nightstand, Lucas poured a good portion of lube onto three fingers then retrieved the candle.

"Pull your legs up."

Kyle obeyed instantly, a mixture of curiosity and apprehension causing a tremor to race through him. Angling an arm in between his raised thighs, Lucas circled a finger around his sensitive entrance then eased it inside. When he felt his muscles relax around the intrusion, another finger was added.

Just as he was beginning to adapt to the stretching, Lucas hooked his fingers and grazed his prostate, pouring a small stream of wax onto his chest at the same time. Pain and pleasure shot through him and he shouted, arching his body involuntarily.

"Hold still, baby."

That was easier said than done. Kyle panted with the effort it took to comply. Each trail of fire on his skin was matched by a stroke along his gland, the combined torture too much and not enough. When the third finger was inserted, he couldn't contain himself any longer. Whimpers and pleas flew from his mouth, though whether he was begging for more pain or pleasure, he wasn't sure. Grabbing onto the bars holding his wrists in place, he used the leverage and slid down to push Lucas' fingers in deeper, desperate to increase the pressure. Tears coated his lashes and overflowed at the physical and emotional onslaught.

In a blur too fast for Kyle to follow, Lucas set the candle aside and replaced his fingers with the tip of his thick cock, forcing Kyle's legs further apart to accommodate his large build. In one swift move, the man plunged in and they both cried out. The intensity of their conjoined emotions swept through him like a tidal wave and it took every ounce of his willpower to keep from coming.

This time Lucas didn't pause for him to adjust to the invasion. He slammed his cock to the root in deep lunges, punishing Kyle's hole in vigorous thrusts. Kyle was beyond words. Every nerve in his body was alight and it felt as though he would fly apart if not for the crushing grip on his thighs. Lucas continued to pummel into him, showing no mercy. Not that he would have asked for it.

Not that he could have.

Just when he thought he couldn't take any more without bursting, Lucas grasped the chain linking the clamps together and yanked them free.

"Come with me!"

Pain and ecstasy charged through him and he exploded, spurting ribbons of cum onto his chest and belly. Lucas slammed into him one last time and roared out his own orgasm. It seemed to last forever, heightening Kyle's pleasure until he thought he might pass out. Finally, Lucas released his legs and eased himself out. The cuffs came next, then Kyle was carried into the bathroom for a shower.

He had just enough strength to stand on his own while Lucas took his time washing the wax and sweat from their bodies. It was so nice to be pampered by someone for a change. No, not just someone. Lucas. There was so much about the man that still remained a mystery. That alone fed his fears. It was time he grabbed his freedom by the balls and took back control.

Or gave it to the gorgeous man doing everything within his power to prove himself.

The idea made his cock stir to life again but he held his arousal in check. As he was being dried off, the irony that sex had now become preferable over talking hit him and he laughed out loud. At Lucas' raised eyebrow, Kyle merely giggled and shook his head.

"Come here, you little imp."

He shrieked as Lucas swept him up and threw him onto the bed then swooped down, tickling and nibbling. Kyle squirmed and shouted in between bursts of laughter. There was no way he could match the man's strength but he didn't necessarily need to. When Lucas had him pinned, Kyle lifted his hips and brought their cocks together, undulating against him. It had the desired effect. As soon as Lucas' eyes glazed, he flipped the big man over and sat on his chest, holding both wrists down in his much smaller hands.

"Hah!" Kyle exclaimed in triumph.

"That's cheating. Sexy as hell but still cheating."

Kyle smirked. "You have your powers, I have mine." He laughed at the mock threat in Lucas' growl and rolled away before they could start in on round two. "Wait, wait, wait. You're distracting me and I...I want to talk." The mood sobered instantly and Lucas moved to lean back against the headboard, giving Kyle a little space, for which he was grateful.

There was still a measure of levity in the air so he decided to begin with an easy topic. "So you like tears, don't you? I noticed that you kinda lost control when you saw them."

"Did I hurt you?"

He waved the man back down when he started to rise. "No, you didn't hurt me. It was..." He cursed his pale skin when blood rushed to his face. "It was really nice."

With a grin, Lucas replied, "Yeah, I like tears, but only the good ones."

Kyle matched his grin, saying, "And I like pain, but only the good kind. Guess that makes us a pretty good match, huh?"

"What are you saying?"

Taking a deep breath, he chose his next words carefully. "Craig never told me he loved me. He called me his addiction. I think I was so desperate to have someone want me that I thought it was love. I had nothing to compare it to. My mom and dad never got along. When Craig became obsessed with controlling everything I did, I started questioning our relationship but I wasn't allowed to talk to anyone about it. Or talk at all." He let out a humourless laugh. "I didn't even know sex could feel good until I had sex with you."

"Making love," Lucas growled. "And no, the act itself should never hurt. He was your first, wasn't he?"

Kyle looked down and nodded. "When you told me about the bond, I thought... I was afraid that you would become like him. That the bond would give you the right to control me like he did."

"Oh sweetness..."

"But I know it's not the same," he ploughed through. If he didn't get everything out now, he wasn't sure he would have the courage to do so later. "Nothing is the same with you. I know you didn't expect us to bond and it took me a while to realise that you wouldn't take advantage of it. So...if you still want me, I'd like to work on it. Maybe make a relationship out of it?" A spike of joy bolted through him as Lucas gathered him into a strong embrace.

"I would love a relationship with you. And once I explain the details of the bonding, you'll know that I will never stop wanting you."

"I think I can live with that kind of obsession. Just one more thing." When Lucas sat back again, Kyle asked, "What's the difference between a submissive and a slave?"

Lucas chuckled. "A slave is essentially what you were, but typically without the abuse. He or she gives their Master complete control over their lives under mutually desired conditions. These are usually outlined in a contract between the two. A submissive and Master can also have a contract, but the conditions are more lenient. For example, I could dominate you in and out of the bedroom and you would be expected to obey my rules, but you would also have the right to negotiate them at any time without reprisal."

Kyle considered the differences for a minute. Where the line was drawn was a little confusing, but one thing stuck out in his mind. There was no abuse. And he trusted Lucas to ensure that. "Can I be your submissive?" This time when Lucas gathered him up, he curled into the large man's arms and stayed there.

"Of course. We can go over the rules and limits, though I don't think a contract will be needed." *"I will always be a part of your life now and I want to deserve that privilege,"* he added through their link. "Now let's take a nap. I'm an old man and you wore me out." Sliding them both beneath the covers, he draped Kyle over his chest and held him close.

Contentment settled into Kyle's entire being, bringing with it a feeling of peace he'd never experienced before. "How old are you?" he asked drowsily.

"Two hundred and fifty-one years last spring."

Kyle shot up only to be dragged down again.

"First rule, you will sleep with me when I'm sleeping. I'm not passing up any chance I get to hold on to you from now on."

With a small grin, Kyle fell asleep to the steady beat of Lucas' heart.

Chapter Six

"How is this?"

Lucas looked up from his laptop to inspect his mate. A black silk shirt, jacket and pants moulded to his small frame, showing off every curve to perfection. The dress shoes bought nearly two weeks ago adorned his feet and his strawberry-blond hair was slicked back into a ponytail. The man looked absolutely stunning. Just as he had the last two times he'd presented himself, but Kyle thrived on compliments so Lucas made sure to give them out...sparingly. In his early years of casual dating, he'd learnt that too many compliments could cheapen the value of one's opinion.

"Turn around."

Kyle huffed but obeyed. While he was faced the other way, Lucas quickly adjusted himself. He knew the lure of a mating was strong, but he had been unprepared for the extreme boost to his libido. They'd been at it like rabbits since Kyle had agreed to accept their bond. Not that he was complaining. If not for his role as Master and proprietor, they'd never leave the bedroom. Or any room in the house for that matter… Occasionally the backyard, depending on the weather of course…

"You look very handsome. Let's head out. Our reservation's in thirty minutes." Lucas stood and held his mate by the arms when he began to grouse. "Behave." Kyle responded by stilling immediately. "You've had a week to prepare for this and I won't allow you to spend the rest of your life in fear. Now get your sweet ass in the car before I have to paddle it." His mate's eyes lit with hope and he couldn't help but to chuckle. "It would be a punishment…and we'd still go out."

Lucas followed the disheartened man out of the house to his Avenger. Kyle was as natural a submissive as they came — obedient with just the right amount of challenge — but this one stipulation Lucas had imposed was proving to be the hardest adjustment for him. It was understandable. No one could blame the man for fearing a chance encounter with his ex.

Lucas was determined, however, to work past this obstacle so that his mate could truly enjoy freedom. Kyle's last excuse for not going out was that he didn't own a suit, to which Lucas had responded by paying a seamstress to make a home visit and take Kyle's measurements to create a tailor-made suit for him.

And damned if it wasn't worth every penny.

He fixed himself again before getting into the car. The sooner they got this over, the sooner they could play with the new toys he'd ordered.

"I'm ready, Sir," Kyle said abruptly.

"Excuse me?"

Turning so that he was facing Lucas as much as the seatbelt would let him, he repeated in a low tone, "I'm ready."

Understanding dawned after a few moments. "What? Now?"

"You said I could ask whenever I wanted to." When Lucas lifted a brow at his defiant tone, he hastily added, "Sir."

It wasn't the most convenient time to answer Kyle's questions about his people and their bond. He would have preferred the intimacy of their home, but he couldn't deny the man's request. Kyle had wanted to take things one step at a time and wait until he felt more comfortable in their relationship before learning more. It looked as though that time was now.

"I did say that, didn't I? All right, what would you like to know first?"

"Are you immortal?"

"No. My people can live for an average of a millennium, barring fatalities and war. Now that we're bonded, you will live for as long as I do, and vice versa."

"So I'm going to live for another eight hundred years? How is that possible?"

"The vibrancy of our souls is what gives my race longevity, as well as advanced strength, speed and occasionally supernatural power. The piece of my soul you took into yourself isn't enough to give you all of these abilities, but it will lengthen your lifespan to match mine."

Kyle thought for a minute then said, "Wait, you said that I'll live for as long as you do. What happens to me if you die?"

And this would be why home would have been preferable.

"When I die, all of my soul dies with me, even the piece inside you. You wouldn't survive it, sweetness. No soul mate can. The same applies to me if you die." Lucas paused to let that sink in. Because of the extensive lifetime of his people, the risk of dying with one's mate was nothing compared to the emptiness of a thousand years spent alone. Most humans, however, cherished their short years too much to sacrifice them for a chance at the type of bond Tsielen were capable of.

When the silence grew too loud, Lucas began, "Baby, I'm really sor—"

"So I guess this means that you can't die, then. Not till we're old and feeble. If you do, I'll haunt you."

Lucas could only stare, open-mouthed, at the smug look on Kyle's face.

"Sir."

He burst out laughing so hard the car swerved.

"Wait, does your kind believe in ghosts?"

When he finally got himself under control, he replied, "No, but I'm sure you'd find a way. We're almost at the restaurant. Did you have any more questions?"

"Tons, but if we only have time for one more until we get back, I want to know what you meant when you said you never wanted to fall in love because of your dangerous past."

Damn, the man had a memory. "That's a rather long story. I promise to tell you at home, okay?" There was a twinge of disappointment from Kyle but he merely nodded and let it go. A valet took the car when they arrived and the maître d' directed them to a private booth reserved for them on the balcony above the main floor. Rolls and wine were served in prelude to the pre-ordered course, but Kyle touched none of it. His mounting nervousness was plain even without the benefit of their bond.

"So ask me another question."

Kyle's head jerked up and he smiled. Throughout the entire meal, Lucas kept him preoccupied with bits of information about his race through their link. It afforded them privacy and to any onlookers, it would appear as though they were simply enjoying each other's company too much for words.

By the time dessert came, the small man was bouncing in his seat, anxious to hear the result of an ancient revolt among his people. When the waitress gave them an odd look, he calmly told his mate to behave and was obeyed instantly. Kyle's submission was always a beautiful thing to witness. It humbled him as much as it gave him pride.

"Shit, hold on baby." He pulled his vibrating phone from his pocket and glanced at the number. It was Amanda's personal cell phone. "Give me one minute." Flipping it open, he said, "Matthews."

Amanda's frantic voice came on the line. "Lucas, sorry if I'm interrupting anything but you need to come down to the store right now. The firemen and police are on their way. I don't know what happened. One second everything was fine and in the next, all hell broke loose!"

"Amanda, slow down. Tell me what happened."

"There's a fire. It started in your office but it's spreading. I can't figure out how it happened."

"All right, we're headed there now. Are you outside? Are you hurt?"

"I'm fine, came outside as soon as I got the customers out."

"Good. Get a good distance away and stay there until help arrives." Lucas hung up, meeting Kyle's troubled gaze. "There's an emergency at the store. I won't have time to drop you off at the house. Will you be okay to come with me?" His mate bravely kept his reluctance from showing.

"Sure."

Lucas flagged down their waitress and paid the bill, tipping her extra to have his car pulled around immediately. The valet driver met them outside shortly afterwards and they climbed in. Fortunately, the store was only a ten minute drive away.

When they arrived, two fire trucks, an ambulance and several police cruisers were barricading the front of the store, forcing him to park at the end of the block. Thick plumes of smoke rose from the vents on the roof of the building and a hose ran through the propped open front doors. Several men had formed a chain to pass crates of alcohol from inside to a safer area.

"I want you to stay here, baby. I need to find Amanda then help with the store. I'll be back as soon as the fire is out, okay?"

Kyle kept his eyes glued on the ordered chaos up ahead, nodding his head absently. As Lucas slid out of the driver's seat, Kyle grabbed his arm and said fiercely, "Be careful." The concern for his welfare warmed him more than he thought could be possible. He planted a light kiss on his mate's forehead then took off in search of Amanda.

She saw him first and came running from the other side of the street, skirting men and vehicles nimbly. For a good-sized woman, she was pretty agile when she wanted to be. Amanda skidded to a halt and he had to brace her to keep her from falling over. Face streaked with tears, she gulped in several breaths to calm herself.

"Lucas, it was an explosion. It sounded like a bomb or something. Your office door flew off and knocked over a shelf. There was liquor everywhere and the flames spread so fast!"

"Was anyone hurt?"

"No, no, but they're still trying to get the fire under control."

The poor woman looked like she was about to shake out of her own skin. Lucas wrapped an arm around her in a partial hug. "You did great. Why don't you go home and drink a cold one. I'll take it from here."

"Are you sure? I can stay if you need me."

A fire breaks out around this woman and she still wants to help those around her. She was absolutely one of a kind. "No. Go on. I'll call you in the morning."

"I already gave my statement to the police. They want one from you, too."

"Thanks, Amanda." He made his way to the chain line and joined in, earning a few sympathetic looks when he informed them that he owned the place. The fire didn't bother him in the least. Money was no object and merchandise could be replaced. What had him pissed off beyond measure was the fact that this could not have been accidental. An electrical short would have started a slow-burning fire but there was nothing in his office that could have caused an explosion.

Five minutes into it, the line broke apart and shortly after that he was asked to speak with an officer. She steered him towards a cruiser parked a short distance away and began with the standard line of questioning. Another officer came over to inform them that the fire was out and an investigation crew would be in as soon as most of the smoke cleared.

"Ma'am, I have suspicions that this was not accidental. I could be wrong but my employee said there was an explosion and I can't think of anything in my office that would warrant that."

The officer nodded grimly. "She reported the same thing to me. Do you know of anyone who might have done this intentionally? Maybe a former employee or enemy of yours?"

Yeah, he did, but damned if he was going to inform her of that. When he found the culprit, he was going to personally ensure the guy never harmed another living being again. "No. I can make a list of my former employees but I doubt any of them would stoop to this. Can you tell me what time this…"

"Lucas!"

The scream reverberated through his head, blocking out all other noise. Fear flooded him so quickly he gasped for air. Then it was gone. The constant presence of his mate in his mind blinked out like the flame of a candle in a gust of wind. The only thing that could sever their link so completely was a state of unconsciousness.

"Kyle!" He shouted, but it was met with absolute silence. Heart pounding, he ran as fast as he could around milling onlookers, shoving people aside and dodging cars. He could see the open passenger door of his Avenger but no one was inside or nearby. Running straight past, he rounded the corner of the block and stopped. There was nothing. No cars or people on either side.

"Kyle!"

His own fear swept in with a vengeance and he raced back to his car to search for clues…but he knew who it was. He'd been at this game for far too long to think it was coincidence. After jumping behind the wheel, he drove as close as he could to the crowd and got out to speak with the same officer. It wouldn't do for them to chase him and witness what he planned on doing to Craig when he caught up with the bastard.

"Mr Matthews?"

"I have another emergency at home. I'll stop in at the station to answer any more questions you have as soon as I can." He ignored her shout as he climbed back into his car and headed towards Craig's house. Rage built inside him until he was almost blind with it. Images of what he was going to do to the man when he got there were the only things that kept the fear at bay.

The mansion was dark as he pulled into the entrance of the driveway. He came to a stop then stealthily made his way around to the rear, putting on a burst of speed. He broke the lock on the handle to the back door and shoved it open as quietly as possible, splintering the wood panelling. There was not a single sound to be heard inside. After leaving his shoes by the door, he began to scout every room, including the basement and attic.

Fear took precedence when he came up empty. The house was utterly vacant.

"*Kyle!*"

Silence.

He could not have beaten them here. Craig had to have had at least a good two to three minute head start on him. Lucas traced his steps back to the desktop he'd seen in the library downstairs. Firing it up, he began hacking into Craig's personal files, reviewing bank statements and personal records until he found what he wanted. The man owned two other properties in this state and one just across the Kansas border.

After jotting down the addresses, he shut off the computer and left through the back door. These were his only leads and until Kyle woke up, they were also his only options.

* * * *

Kyle awoke to the feel of his skull splitting in two. Bright lights above pierced his eyes when he cracked them open, making him flinch. Every muscle in his body ached and his stomach threatened to lose its contents at any moment. Bringing his hands to his face, he realised they were cuffed in front, as well as his ankles.

"Kyle!"

"Good, you're finally awake."

Both voices hit him simultaneously and his head reeled. When the room finally stopped spinning, he opened his eyes once more, blinking rapidly against the glare of the lights. Finely meshed walls encased him, digging into the bare skin on his right side. Beyond them, Craig sat complacently on a tall barstool a few yards away. Tools and shelves of car parts adorned the walls while various odds and ends cluttered the floor.

He knew this place. Had been in this very room with Craig countless times in the past but his mind was still too groggy to function properly.

"Baby, tell me where you are."

The warmth that flowed in was swallowed whole by his fear. Hanging on to the echo of Lucas' voice like a lifeline, his mind scrambled to recall his location. His concentration broke as Craig stood and walked forwards.

"I think it's about time we began your lesson, don't you?"

Kyle whimpered as the man approached with a malicious sneer. After unlocking the small door, Craig yanked him out of the dog crate by his hair and stood him up. His knees refused to support him and he snatched weakly at the arm holding him to ease the pain in his scalp.

"Lucas, I'm...I'm..."

Craig hauled him to the middle of the room and lifted him by the elbows. The silver cuffs around his wrists were latched onto a rusted, metal hook attached to the ceiling, suspending him in the air.

"Did you honestly think you could get away from me?" Rearing back, Craig cracked his palm across Kyle's face. "It wasn't hard to surmise that the asshole who stole you from me was keeping you hidden. He hasn't been back to work since that day." Crushing Kyle's jaw in a tight grip, he hissed, "You should have come back to me."

When the man turned and strode over to a bench, Kyle searched his memory desperately. Lucas' deep, commanding voice poured into him like a soothing balm.

"I know you're scared, sweetness. Do what I taught you and push past your fear. I can be there in seconds once you tell me where you are. You will obey me and calm yourself."

He would obey. He would abide by his Master's rules. He would not allow this maniac to control him. Kyle repeated the words Lucas had told him the day they'd both accepted their bond. They came to him as clearly as though his mate were in the room with him and gave him strength.

"Highway 54..."

"Last time I used the whip, but that obviously wasn't enough. If there's one thing I admire about you, it's that you help me to come up with new and inventive forms of punishment." Craig picked up what appeared to be a small electric shock device. "I think I'll save this for last." Placing it on the stool, he went for a large, wooden paddle with several small holes in the middle.

Kyle's breathing quickened. *"State Highway K. Lucas, please hurry."*

Craig came forwards again, grinning evilly. "Sometimes I love it when you defy me. It gives me a chance to exercise my little sadistic pleasures."

When the man disappeared behind him, Kyle started to hyperventilate.

"That's good, baby. I know where that is. Just give me a little more information."

Then it came to him. He knew exactly where he was. *"I'm four miles – "* Blazing pain cut off his sentence as the paddle came down hard on his ass. A scream was ripped from his throat and by the time his breath ran out, Craig had landed four more blows. The man was relentless, striking him again and again, each one harder than the last. The pain was so intense it stole the very air from Kyle's lungs. His thoughts scattered into a million fragments until all that existed was the fire in his backside.

He wasn't sure when it ended but Lucas' voice managed to break through his fever of agony.

"Four miles which way, baby. North or south?"

Through the sheen of tears, he watched Craig approach with a single-tail whip in hand. *"South! A cabin down the first road on the right. Lucas!"*

"When this is over, you will learn your place. No more..."

There was a loud crash upstairs and Craig span around in time to see the basement door fly from its hinges. Kyle was only able to catch a glimpse of Lucas before everything became a blur. The sounds of fighting and objects shattering lasted only seconds, then he was being lifted again and lowered into a familiar embrace.

"It's okay, baby. I've got you. Close your eyes for me."

He was too weak to do anything but follow orders. There was an odd sensation of displacement then Lucas was laying him down on a soft bed. Opening his eyes, he realised they were at home in their bedroom. Lucas tucked a finger from each hand into the cuff on one wrist and broke it apart. The same was repeated to the cuffs on his other wrist and ankles.

"Turn over, sweetness. Let me see your back."

When he complied, a barrage of emotions blasted him. Anger, guilt, torment and more bowled into him, shredding the last of his defences and causing sobs to wrack his body without respite. The powerful blast of Lucas' emotions dimmed but he was helpless to stop the torrent of anguish that flowed from his body in tears and choking whimpers. Through it all, Lucas held and rocked him, murmuring words of comfort.

When at last the floodgates ran dry and the violent quaking faded, a soft cloth wiped his eyes and Lucas' handsome features came into view. Nothing had ever looked so wonderful.

"I need to pack some bags then we're going to take a little trip. A vacation, so to speak. Try to get some sleep and I'll be right back for you."

Kyle didn't want to let go, but his energy had fled with his tears and his lids closed of their own accord.

Chapter Seven

Heat blanketed every inch of his skin, infusing his pores and enveloping him in a tight cocoon. It was peaceful here, relaxing. Which meant that his mate was with him. He squirmed to dig an arm from the layers surrounding him when Lucas' hand moved from his waist to his hair.

"Shhh, I'm right here. You're safe now. Try to go back to sleep."

Low vibrations and the cool tone of Lucas' voice nearly pulled him under again but his bladder had other plans in mind. "Umm...Sir, I have to pee."

Threading his hand through the strands of Kyle's hair, Lucas said, "We'll pull in for the night at the town up ahead. Can you wait ten minutes?"

Kyle nodded and burrowed his face in what he discovered was the man's lap. The position put ideas in his head that he couldn't resist. He nudged his nose deep into Lucas' crotch, rubbing along the lengthening column and inhaling the scent of musk mixed with laundry detergent.

"Behave, imp," Lucas growled softly. "We're almost there."

He snuggled in with a few more nudges then settled down. A short while later, Lucas parked the car and told him to stay put. In no time his mate came back and pulled the car around a corner.

"Let me get our bag and open the door. Don't move."

"Where are we?"

"I'll explain after I get you in the room."

Frowning, Kyle waited for the man to return. In the span of two blinks, Lucas was leaning over his head and picking him up. They entered what could only be a hotel room, with puke-worthy paisley curtains that matched the bedspread. The moment his behind touched the bed, he cried out in surprise and pain. Flashes of events filtered through his mind in a jumbled mess.

"Craig found me — how did he know I was there?"

Lucas kept his expression impassive as he tucked a pillow under Kyle's head then rummaged through a duffel bag on the floor. "Either he, or someone he paid off, set the fire in the store. Craig knew you were staying with me and took a chance on you coming with me to investigate." A small tube was pulled from the bag and he set it aside in order to unravel Kyle from the blankets wrapped around him.

"He took me to his father's cabin. I remember you asking me where it was, and then you were there."

Cotton pants and a sweatshirt were peeled off next. "Lay down, sweetness." He squeezed a dollop of cream into his palm. "This will help with the bruising."

The urge to obey warred with defiance but he eventually gave in to the command. "How did you get there so fast?" The cream felt cool on his burning skin and a small moan slipped out.

"We can talk about this in the morning after we get some rest."

Kyle twisted to send Lucas a glare. "I feel like I've slept for days. Any more rest and I'll slip into a coma. I need answers now." A smart smack on the side of his thigh was enough to remind him of his role. "Sorry, Sir. Can we please discuss this before going to bed?"

There was a loud sigh behind him. "Can you stand?"

It damn sure didn't feel like it, but he gave it a shot. Once on his feet, Lucas clasped his hips from behind and guided him to the bathroom. Each step made his backside throb and he had to bite his lip to keep from voicing his agony. It was awkward, trying to take a piss while being held from behind, but he was grateful for the support.

Back in the room, his mate helped him under the covers. "I need to take a shower first then we'll talk about what happened." A hoagie, chips and a bottle of water sat on the nightstand near his head. "For now, try to eat. It's been about twenty-four hours since you've had food in your stomach."

Nodding, he leaned into the kiss on his temple. With the first bite, his appetite roared back to life. It wasn't long before three empty containers lay discarded on the stand and he discovered that lying on a full belly was less than comfortable. The bathroom door opened and his hot, heavily muscled saviour came out in nothing but a low-slung white towel highlighting an exquisitely rounded butt. Craning his neck to eye the succulent view, Kyle forgot all pain and rolled over.

"Ouch!"

Lucas whipped around and Kyle felt his face flame. Rolling back, he took refuge in the depths of the pillow.

"Are you okay?"

"Yeah, yeah. Nothing to see here, just...go away." A soft chuckle reached his ears that didn't help matters. By the time the bed dipped under Lucas' weight, Kyle thought it was safe to come out again.

"How are you feeling?"

Compared to what he would be feeling had Lucas not rescued him? Great. Peachy. "Better." A hint of hesitancy flitted into Kyle so he decided not to push the issue of his question.

"Do you recall what I said about the particular attributes of Tsielen?"

"Strength and speed."

"And occasionally other powers. I can teleport to any known location at any time."

"So when I told you where I was, you teleported there?"

Lucas nodded.

Kyle digested this information for a bit. It would explain the man's sudden appearance and their subsequent arrival in their bedroom. Truthfully, he thought it was possibly the coolest power in the world, but apparently Lucas had felt the need to keep it a secret. Pieces of the puzzle were still missing.

"What happened to Craig?"

"He's no longer an issue."

"Sir, what did you do? Is that why we're at a hotel, because we're running?"

Lucas fixed him with a piercing blue gaze. "He was still breathing when we left. Whether or not he lives long enough for someone to find him is not my responsibility. And no, that's not why we're running."

"So this really isn't a vacation." It wasn't a question and he received no answer. Amanda's earlier words came back to him about loneliness. Lucas had proved himself time and again and yet he still felt the need to hide parts of his life. There was only one reason Kyle could think of for that and the possibility floored him.

Willing to test any theory to get the man to open up, Kyle scooted over and rested his head in Lucas' lap, facing him. "I won't leave you, Sir. No matter what you tell me, I'm here, and I'm staying here. Bonding with you has been the best thing that's ever happened to me and nothing you say can change that."

Lucas stared at him for the longest time as though frozen in contemplation. Abruptly, he bent over and kissed him desperately. *"I don't deserve you."*

"I could say the same."

That brought out the intended laugh and both relaxed into their previous positions. Lucas adapted a reminiscent look and said, "My race has an Order called the Mackaeo, much like your police force. They patrol the activities of all Tsielen on Earth and have the authority to punish those who break our rules. Depending on the offence, the criminal will either become an indentured servant to the Queen and her extended family or be condemned to die.

"The Mackaeo are made up of those Tsielen who are born with a power. It gives them certain advantages over others, enabling them to apprehend criminals easily. I was taken from my family at the age of ten, when my power first showed itself. Because my power is rare and favourable when conducting hunts, I was trained to track down those with a death sentence and carry it out."

"You were a trained killer?" Kyle tried to keep the amazement out of his voice. It was disturbing yet thrilling in a perverse sort of way to know that his mate really could protect him at all costs.

"For over two centuries. I didn't mind my job so much. I've seen what a rogue Tsielen can do when a member of the Mackaeo fails to bring them to justice."

"But you quit."

"No," Lucas said quietly. "There is no quitting the Mackaeo. I left because some of the members were becoming corrupt. A select group decided to take it upon themselves to seize lands and funds from humans all in the name of the Queen. Those who found out about us because of their carelessness were murdered. I couldn't be a part of that."

Kyle frowned. "Does your Queen condone this?"

"She is completely unaware of it. When the Mackaeo are sent to kill a Tsielen, they confiscate all of the criminal's monetary possessions and give fifty per cent to the Queen. Last I heard they were giving an additional twenty per cent of what they gained from humans as well. They keep the rest to split amongst themselves and the Queen thinks they're doing a better job taking care of criminals based on the increase in income."

"I still don't understand why we're on the run."

With a sigh, Lucas caressed his cheek. "A few Mackaeo have the ability to sense when others use their power. Because I used mine to find you, they'll try to track me down and force me to join them. I was the only member in The Order with the ability to teleport and with my power they could probably double their revenues. It took me four years to shake them when I left. It shouldn't take that long to lose them this time, though. I've been making preparations for this type of emergency for years."

Kyle opened his mouth again but Lucas stayed his next question with a kiss. It was so full of longing and passion that he knew he'd been right. This big, intimidating, glorious specimen of a man — *Tsielen* — was scared of losing him. The thought aroused him more than any compliment Lucas had given him to date.

His cock swelled and he massaged it along a firm thigh. Lucas took it in hand and began stroking him in long, steady pulls. The kiss deepened and he moaned into the mouth devouring him. This was worth everything he'd gone through in life. The insufferable years of heartache, pain and isolation had all led him to this point, this man. His Master could be gentle and sweet, or exciting and rough. He loved it all. When his balls tightened and he teetered precariously on the brink of release, Lucas circled his thumb and forefinger just beneath the rim of the head and applied enough pressure to deny his orgasm.

"This is off-limits until I give you permission to come." At Kyle's whine, he increased the pressure.

"Yes, Sir," he said breathlessly.

"Very good. Now let's get some sleep. We have a long day tomorrow." Lucas positioned him across his chest then was out in seconds.

The next few hours spent trying to follow his Master's command and ignore his throbbing hard-on redefined the meaning of the word torture for him.

* * * *

Lucas cast another sidelong glance at his mate. Kyle had been distant and quiet for most of the day, his moods fluctuating between depressed and irritated, and now sullen. Considering the latest incident with Craig, it was understandable, but he didn't know how much more he could take of his mate's withdrawal.

He would always live with the shame and guilt of breaking his promise of safety. It was his burden to bear. Kyle, however, should not have to suffer for something he'd been powerless to prevent. Of course there was the option of professional help, though he hoped it didn't come to that. As far as he knew, he was the only person Kyle had opened up to since his mom had died.

"Baby, nothing that happened was your fault. If you're worried about Craig, I can send an anonymous call to the police and have a cruiser sent out to the cabin."

Kyle gave him an incredulous look. "What? No! I hope that prick rots in hell. I hope he spends eternity kissing the devil's ass and shovelling crap. I hope..."

"Okay, okay. I think I get the picture. Damn boy, I don't think I've ever been prouder."

"Low-life, rotten, slimy scum-sucking piece of..."

"And changing the subject. If that's not what's bothering you, what is?"

Thinning his lips, Kyle gazed out of the window. "Will we ever go back home?"

So that's what this was about. Kyle was giving up everything he'd known to run with him. Granted there wasn't much of a choice. If the Mackaeo found out Lucas had a mate, they would use Kyle to lure him out. Still, he hadn't taken the time to realise how hard this must be for Kyle.

"No. I ported from there so they'll find out it's mine and seize it."

"What about the store?"

"They'll track that to me, too. They won't be able to access my accounts but most likely they'll try to sell it. I'll set up arrangements for Amanda and the others to work for a few business associates I know if they want to."

Kyle paused then said, "This is my fault. You have to leave your home, your business and friends, all because of me."

He'd been wrong on both counts. Eventually he'd figure out his mate, but apparently it wouldn't be today. "Sweetness, I took the risk of this happening long before I met you. It was very possible when I left the Mackaeo that I would have to run for the rest of my life. After I managed to hide myself, the only reason I bought the house and created my business was to stave off boredom. Eight hundred years of sitting on my ass and spending my wealth isn't exactly appealing from my perspective. What I've lost is nothing compared to what I've gained. Do you understand?"

A shy smile lifted Kyle's soft lips. "Yes, Sir."

"Good, because I'd hate to have to restrict you from the playroom when we get there."

"Get where?"

"One of my other houses."

"It has a playroom?" Kyle bounced once then yelped.

"Down boy, and yes, there's a playroom. I'll give you a few days to heal then show you."

The most adorable little pout played across Kyle's face. "That's just wrong. You tell me about it then make me wait?"

"Don't worry. I have other plans for you." An hour later they arrived at the house. Lucas had to pick up Kyle's chin when they spotted it.

"*This* is yours?"

Lucas scanned the building and surrounding lawns. Everything seemed in order. "Yeah. I'll have to talk to the lawn maintenance guy about cutting back some of the trees but I can't see anything else wrong."

"It looks like a castle. This is so awesome!" Kyle climbed out as soon as the car came to a halt and started exploring as fast as his bruised body would let him. Joining him, Lucas also took the time to admire the appeal of the house.

Large black rocks had been cut in half and sanded so that the flat sides lay flush with the outer brick walls and the rounded sides stuck out. Mortar held them in place along the entire outer surface, giving the appearance of a house made completely from stone. Two parapets towered ten feet above the roof on either side in the front and two more, slightly taller, stood up in the back. The windows were narrow and pointed at the top with cast iron frames and the front doors were thick enough to hinder a battering ram.

He had a penchant for gothic styles and this house had been too good to pass on. The interior had required a lot of reconstruction but looking at the place now, he didn't regret a dime. When Kyle gasped as he bent over to get a closer view of the flowering vines, Lucas took his hand and led him to the doors.

"You can explore the grounds later. I need to make a phone call then apply more cream to your backside." The doors slid open easily and he was no less impressed with the upkeep of the interior. He'd have to call the cleaning crew to cancel this week's maintenance to afford them some privacy. All of the decorations and furniture were either gothic or antique, the only modern appliances being his computer and those occupying the kitchen.

At the claw foot sofa couch, he lay Kyle down and threw the quilt from the back over him. "I'll grab the bags and be right in."

"Did you bring the laptop?"

"Yes, it'll be the first thing I bring in." Lucas tucked him in and closed the doors on his way out. Pulling his cell phone from his pocket, he dialled Bastian.

"Whoever you are, you've got the wrong phone number."

"Hello to you too, sunshine."

"Deluc?"

"It's me. I need a favour."

Bastian growled into the phone. "Seriously? You're gone for more than five years and call me out of the blue when I'm about to get laid? Damn, you've got some timing."

With a smirk, he unloaded the trunk. It was good to know there were still constants in life. The sun coming up, seasons changing, and Bastian trying to get laid every chance he got. "Put your dick back in your pants."

"Hold on, it's gonna take me a while to get the beast back in there."

Lucas rolled his eyes. In the background he could hear a woman's shrill voice gradually rising, most likely with every excuse Bastian gave her. After the sound of a door slamming, the man came back on the phone.

"Great, thanks. Now what can my blue balls help you with?"

"Do you still have a few of the false identities and account numbers I left with you?"

"Sure. What's up?"

"Take the one of Jonathan Smith and buy a new car, something that can hold a lot of luggage. I'll also need you to keep tabs on a liquor store I own in Ballwin, Missouri, under the name of Lucas Matthews. Check police records and the county clerk's office for anyone that might enquire about repossessing the property. Next check the local hospital and morgue records for a Craig Morgan. If he's dead, I'll need the police file on him."

"So I take it this isn't a social visit?"

"I had to use my power so they'll be on me again. We'll be staying here for about a week then moving on."

"Shit, man, what were you thinking? It took you four years to lose them last time."

"I'm better prepared now." He ignored the loud snort on the other end. "Buy some groceries, too. Make sure you get pancake mix, Texas bread and some fruit."

"Anything else, your highness?"

"Nah, but I'll think of something later."

He hung up, smiling at Bastian's string of epithets. There wasn't a thing in the world they wouldn't do for each other, but cock-blocking the man was tantamount to ripping a leg off…and he took joy in it every time. Picking up one of the bags and the laptop case, he brought them in to Kyle, advising him to only watch movies and not to contact anyone.

"No friends, remember?"

Lucas perched on the edge of the couch and ran his fingers through the man's golden hair. "When this is over, I promise we'll fix that. You can work on your diploma and start college. We can move anywhere you want."

"I don't want anywhere, I just want you." The sincerity in his eyes echoed the honesty Lucas felt thrumming from the piece of Kyle's soul inside him.

An unfamiliar ache clogged his throat and he tried to clear it without success. "I brought some DVDs," he said, handing the case to his mate. "Take your pants off so I can put more medicine on you."

"You don't have to, Sir. I can do it."

"No," he snapped. At Kyle's reactive flinch, he closed his eyes and silently berated himself. In truth, he hated having to apply the bruising cream twice a day. The proof of his failure marked in angry black and purple bruises cut him more effectively than any finely honed blade. During his career as an assassin, not a single innocent human or Tsielen had been harmed by his targets once he was assigned to take them out. And yet, he hadn't been able to protect the one being that had come to mean the most to him.

Tightening the fist he kept on his self-contempt and guilt, Lucas focused on the feelings Kyle was emitting and to his relief there was no fear, only hurt. Not good by far, but an improvement. Opening his eyes, he saw that Kyle had his face tucked into his crossed arms.

"Look at me, baby." Kyle complied with an ounce of trepidation. "I'm sorry. You didn't deserve that, but as your Dom it's my job to take care of you, especially when this could have been prevented." Stopping the young man's protest with a finger, he said, "Don't argue with your Master. Now show me your backside."

The tension in Kyle's muscles gradually faded as he spread the cream over his battered cheeks. The swelling had gone down but it would still be a few weeks at least before he could enjoy paddling and whipping the sweet ass...if ever. Kyle had shown enthusiasm over the prospect of making use of the playroom while they were here, but whether he would be able to handle being struck again, even in a sexual context, remained to be seen.

After screwing the cap back on, he draped the blanket over Kyle once more and set the laptop on the glass top coffee table nearby. "I'm going to bring in the rest of the luggage and make a few phone calls. There won't be any food in the fridge until tomorrow so I was thinking about ordering pizza. Sound good?"

"Yes, Sir. Can we get Hawaiian and breadsticks?"

"Sure. Whatever you want." As he moved to stand, a small hand on his held him back. "What is it, sweetness?"

"Are we moving here?"

Thankfully, he felt no blame or insecurity in Kyle's emotions, only curiosity. "No, we have to keep moving for a bit to make sure we aren't being followed." Kyle nodded, seemingly unperturbed. Lucas moved but was again pulled back down.

"Are you going to call Amanda?"

"Yes, I was planning on it."

"Can you tell her she was right, and that I said thank you?"

Lucas furrowed his brow but Kyle merely grinned and popped a movie into the laptop.

Chapter Eight

The next morning, Kyle awoke to a string of soft kisses along his jaw and neck. Sighing into them, he turned towards Lucas only to whine when the man moved out of his reach. He opened his eyes and saw that Lucas was fully dressed in his usual black attire with a jacket on.

"Get up, baby. I want you to meet a friend of mine before I head to the bank."

Kyle rubbed the sleep from his eyes and sat up. "We're going out?"

"I am. I want you to stay off your feet as much as possible to help the bruises fade."

"You're leaving me alone with someone?" The thought sent a shiver down his spine. It dawned on him that they'd not spent a moment apart since the day Lucas had originally rescued him, but for Craig's latest—and hopefully last—attack. That, coupled with the idea of being left alone with a stranger, had his heart thumping in his chest.

"Not just someone. I've known him for two and a half centuries and he's the only one I would trust with your safety. Get dressed and meet me downstairs." Lucas bent to tuck a lock of his hair behind one ear then left, closing the door on his way out.

With a groan Kyle slipped from the bed and took a quick shower. The trust Lucas had in his friend dispelled some of his doubts, but not all. He wasn't sure when he'd become so dependent on the man. Even prior to the reassuring connection of their bond, Lucas' strong confidence had given him a measure of his own. The shame he'd first felt at constantly needing to rely on the man instead of his own independence had disappeared some time ago. Putting his welfare and faith into the hands of his Master was as natural to him now as breathing.

Choosing a sedate outfit from one of the duffels, he made his way slowly down the wine-coloured, carpeted stairs and found Lucas talking with another man in the kitchen. The stranger was fairly handsome with short, brown curls and a build slightly leaner than Lucas'. His baggy plaid shorts and white button-up shirt topped with a black tie looked more like a fashion statement than a casual state of dress.

As he walked into the room, both men stopped talking and turned to him. Light brown eyes crinkled from the smile on the stranger's face that would have been warm if not for the thin edge to it. Kyle got the distinct impression that the man didn't quite approve of his presence.

Lucas went to him immediately and placed a hand on his shoulder. "Bastian, this is Kyle. Kyle, Bastian. He'll be staying with you while I'm out. The groceries," he said, indicating the numerous plastic bags in a corner of the room with a wave of his hand, "need to be put away. After that I want you to lie down. Bastian can show you where I keep my books if you want to read or you can watch more movies on the laptop but make sure you sit and stand as little as possible."

"Yes, Sir. How long will you be?" He couldn't resist casting a sideward glance at Bastian.

"Not too long. I'm just going to the bank then picking up more medicine for you. Town is only a ten minute drive from here."

He bravely drew himself up and stifled the temptation to beg Lucas to take him along. One of the rules that had been set down at the beginning of their relationship was that Kyle would refrain from disputing any commands that were directly related to his health. It was originally meant to give Lucas the additional authority to determine how much he ate at each meal, which he didn't mind so much, but now it was just damned annoying.

"Behave while I'm gone and don't forget to eat breakfast."

"Yes, Sir," he replied, not quite able to keep the disappointment he felt from his tone. Lucas grinned knowingly then pecked him on the forehead before heading out. Kyle got to work on filling the cabinets and fridge with the groceries. To his utter relief, he found that the kitchen was filled with modern appliances and cookware. He was used to going without television and other such luxuries, but when it came to cooking, he preferred to take full advantage of modern conveniences.

Bastian's eyes tracked his every action. It was uncomfortable to say the least. The charge of tension that filled the air kept him from wanting to strike up a conversation, and the man certainly wasn't putting forth the effort, so he remained quiet. Lucas hadn't specified what or how much he had to eat for breakfast so Kyle took an apple out when he was finished.

Going into the living room to retrieve the laptop, he heard Bastian walking behind him. To say he was creeped out would be an understatement. The urge to reach out through the link just to hear Lucas' reassuring voice was strong but he held it in. The friendship between Bastian and Lucas was obviously important to his lover and he didn't want jeopardise that by appearing wary of the stranger.

Snatching the laptop and case, Kyle let out a relieved sigh when Bastian stayed at the foot of the stairs, watching him ascend to the bedroom. Once inside, he closed the door and plopped onto the bed, grateful for the small degree of privacy. Thirty minutes into the movie he was watching, movement caught his attention out of the corner of his eye. Glancing up, he jerked upright and scrambled to the head of the bed.

Bastian stood with his arms folded across his chest and feet apart, a cocky look plastered on his face. Kyle glanced at the still-closed door then back at him. He was sure he would have heard or seen the man come in. Another push with his legs brought his back against the headboard, and that still wasn't enough distance between them for Kyle's peace of mind.

"So you must be the reason Deluc used his power."

Kyle frowned, caught off-guard. "Deluc?"

"You probably know him by some other name since he was trying to keep his whereabouts hidden. Guess that's pointless now, but hey, it's only four years of running down the drain. Six years of rest and relaxation brought to a bitter end. He's tough, though. He'll get through this. No skin off your back, right? When he's done going through the trouble of making sure you're not killed in the process, you can go on your merry way knowing that your precious little life is safe."

The sarcastic note in Bastian's voice shook him as much as his words.

"What's another four years of fleeing for his life compared to more than two hundred years of being required to kill his own kind? Oh, that's right. You probably can't even imagine the hell he's gone through to protect your people and ours. You're young, sexy and enjoying the fringe benefits of rich men like him. I can't blame him, really. You are a hot piece of ass. Tell you what, after you're done screwing with him, you can stay with me until it's safe to get back to your plush life."

Bastian advanced with a malicious gleam in his eyes. "I'd fuck you in a heartbeat, but I'm not as generous as Deluc. You'd leave with only what you came with." Two more steps brought him to the side of the bed, leaving only a few feet of distance between them. "I can tell you're a submissive. Deluc is a great Dom but he's not the only one. I can guarantee you'd be satisfied every day with what I could do to you."

Terror gripped Kyle's heart and he bolted from the room, narrowly avoiding Bastian's outstretched hand. By the time he hefted the front door open, tears blurred his vision but that didn't matter. What mattered was the fact that the house was located a good distance from any surrounding neighbours. No one would hear his screams for help if Bastian chose to make good on his threat.

"Kyle?"

For the first time since meeting Lucas, the man's deep voice caused something other than succour to fill him.

Panic and turmoil crashed through Kyle like an avalanche. He couldn't let his mate find out about Bastian's harsh words. It would kill their friendship and Lucas would grow to despise him for it.

"Kyle, tell me what's going on now."

A sob hitched in his chest but he kept running. There was no good way for this to end. Disobeying his Master went against all of his instincts. Lucas would be furious with him when he got home. Even if the man didn't hit him, his censure would be enough to hurt Kyle more than any instrument of pain could. Suddenly, Bastian appeared in front of him and he skidded to a halt too abruptly. Losing his balance, he cried out as he fell roughly onto his behind.

"Afraid I can't let you get away, sweetheart. As much as I'd like to see justice done and watch you pay for putting my friend's life in danger, Deluc charged me with keeping your ass safe. So let's play nice and head back to the house."

Anger broke through the fear and Kyle wanted to spit in his face when they were interrupted by the ringtone of Bastian's cell phone. The man dug it from his pants pocket and answered, keeping his gaze levelled on Kyle. Kyle glared back, fuming from his position on the ground.

"He's right here. We were just having a pleasant conversation." There was a short pause, then, "Yeah, he's fine." After another pause, the man said, "I didn't say anything to intentionally upset him. I was just telling it like it is." Bastian's face paled significantly with whatever words came from Lucas next. "How...how do you know he's scared?"

"Because he's my mate!"

Lucas yelled into the phone so loudly that Kyle was able to discern every word with crystal clarity. Bastian's eyes went wide with shock.

"Oh…fuck. Deluc, I'm so sorry. I had no idea. I…" Lucas must have cut him off because Bastian nodded briskly then hung up the phone a few seconds later. "Kyle, please forgive me."

Bastian took a step forwards and Kyle retreated. His ass was aching viciously but he pushed the pain from his mind. Though the look of regret shining from the stranger's eyes seemed sincere, Kyle wasn't about to trust the man. Neither could he give in to the emotions of anger and worry coursing through him from Lucas. Bastian may have come across as a complete asshole but his words rang true. They mimicked the very concerns he had expressed to Lucas the day before.

"Deluc is on his way. Please come back to the house with me where I can apologise properly. You have every right to hate me and I swear I won't touch you if you don't want me to." He walked several yards to the side so that he was neither ahead of nor behind Kyle. "Shit, you're shaking like a leaf." Dragging a hand through his curls, Bastian mumbled, "Deluc is going to kill me for this."

The wide gap that now separated them did nothing to ease his anxiety. The man had proved he could teleport and from what Kyle knew of the power, it meant that Bastian could catch him no matter how far away he was. Getting to his feet, he winced as blood rushed to his bruises. They walked back to the house together, Kyle stiffly and Bastian eyeing him yet again, only with concern instead of his earlier veiled contempt. Kyle stopped at the top of the porch steps and leaned against a side beam for support.

"Don't want to go inside with me? Okay, I get that." Bastian stayed in the yard, stuffing his hands in his pockets. "I know you must think I'm a total jackass. Deluc is going to rip me a new one for this, so before I die a very painful and humiliating death, I want to say again that I truly am sorry. I love that man like a brother and I let my fear for him cloud my judgement. It's hard for Tsielen to find a soul mate, the one person they want to spend the rest of their life with. But for Deluc…I never thought it would happen. He deserves it, though. More than anyone I know."

Kyle watched him warily, anxious and full of dread for when Lucas would get back. If his mate asked him about what happened, he wouldn't be able to lie, but the truth might drive a wedge between the two friends. The thought that he would be responsible for taking away another aspect of Lucas' life tore at his insides.

Bastian's voice carried, though he spoke quietly. "For what it's worth, thank you. There isn't anything I wouldn't do to find the one person willing to share their soul with me, and I'm glad Deluc found you."

* * * *

Lucas pulled up to the house and jumped out of the new Chevy Tahoe Bastian had purchased for him. Kyle leaned against a pillar at the top of the steps, looking exhausted and utterly still, but his emotions were a riot. The skittish look in his shaded eyes, the one that he had worked so hard to abolish, sliced through him. When he reached the bottom stair and placed one foot on it, Kyle took a step back.

"Easy baby. You know I won't hurt you."

Kyle shook his head. His cheeks were streaked with tears though his eyes were dry.

"You think I'm going to be upset with you?" At his mate's hesitant nod, Lucas sighed. *"I'm pretty sure that's impossible. I don't know what went on or how Bastian fucked up so royally in less than an hour, but we'll make this right. You have to trust me."*

Lucas waited patiently, giving him the control to decide when and if he was ready to accept support. Kyle needed to be reminded that he had options. Two weeks of thriving as a submissive could not erase five years of enforced slavery. He would get there eventually. The man had a reserve of strength that was astonishing, but he often let his fear supersede it along with everything else.

Kyle flicked a surreptitious glance at Bastian's lone form across the lawn, then flung himself into Lucas' arms. His body trembled slightly and Lucas poured all of his relief and pride into his mate.

"I'm sorry, Sir."

"Shhh. You've done very well. You conquered your fear and put your faith in me. A master couldn't ask for any treasure in a sub more beautiful than that. My power over you is nothing without your willingness and trust. Never forget that, sweetness." Kyle nodded and held on tighter. *"Let's get you inside and into bed. You need rest and I have a few choice words to say to Bastian."*

"Please don't get mad at him. He was only trying to look out for you. It wasn't his fault."

Lucas creased his forehead and tried to look down but Kyle had a death grip on him. He bent to swing his mate up into his hold and was met at the front door by Bastian, who opened it then stood aside. Ignoring the man, he carried Kyle to the bedroom. After tucking him into bed and assuaging his frayed nerves until his mate was fast asleep, Lucas went back downstairs and found his friend in the living room. Bastian held two glasses and handed one to him. Lucas sniffed at it, recognising the scent of the special reserve brandy he kept in his liquor cabinet.

Bastian shrugged at his raised brow. "Can't blame a guy for trying to increase his chances at living."

The man had a point. Downing the contents, he traded his empty glass for the other one Bastian handed him and took a seat in the armchair while his friend got a drink for himself. Lucas held his tongue as Bastian sat across from him. His friend stared into the golden liquid in his glass for several moments before looking up at him.

"I knew he was the reason for why you used your power. I thought he was just some guy and I was angry that you would throw away your freedom to help out a human who I thought had no comprehension of what you'd sacrificed."

Bastian took a sip, contemplating his next words. "In a moment of sheer stupidity, I blamed him and said some things you would probably castrate me for. There's no excuse for my behaviour." Leaning forwards to stand, he said, "Let's get this over with before I drink too much. You've got one hell of a punch and I don't want to puke my guts up."

"Sit down. As much as I'd love to kick your ass right now, I promised my mate I wouldn't."

Bastian paused in confusion. "You did? Why?"

"Because he doesn't think I should blame you. Said that you were only trying to protect me. For whatever reason, he disobeyed me by not answering me through the link just to save your sorry ass from my anger." Dumbfounded, his friend could only gape at him. "I suppose I should have told you that he was my mate, but then again, I expected you to treat anyone I would willingly give over to you for protection with respect."

Bastian was the picture of contrition. "You're absolutely right. Wow, he really tried to defend me? You've got one hell of a mate. Not that I particularly want a beating, but damn. Where the hell did you find him?"

Lucas sighed, willing himself to let go of some of the wrath still pumping through his veins. He had no doubt that his friend had his best interests in mind, but the man could be denser than a brick at times. "He worked for me at my store. One day he called in and quit. I went to his house and found him locked in a closet, practically half dead. His boyfriend and brother had been keeping him as an abused slave for five years."

"Mother fucker," Bastian whispered.

"I took him home and the first time we made love, he cared about me so much that he gave me his soul without even realising it." Lucas cleared his hoarse throat. "His ex set fire to my store to distract me long enough to kidnap Kyle after that. Even using my power, though, it wasn't enough. I got there before the man killed him but not before he…" Taking a deep breath to regain control of his broiling emotions, he said harshly, "The guy was going to use a Taser on him after he was done beating him. Kyle wouldn't have survived."

Neither one spoke for a long time. Finally, Bastian rose to refill their drinks. "I accused him of being a spoilt little human. I couldn't have been more wrong. There's got to be some way I can fix my mistake. I'll do anything. Does he like games? Computers?"

"He's been living in forced seclusion since he was sixteen. Electronics don't really mean that much to him right now."

"Well there went my pride for the next decade."

"Look, the man knows the difference between good and bad. He didn't give a flying fuck about whether I left his ex alive or not but he stood up for you despite your epic fail. If he hasn't already forgiven you, he will. The only thing you can do now is show him that he doesn't have to be afraid of you."

Nodding grimly, Bastian swallowed his shot. "I can do that. You know I'd do anything to help you, but I want you to know that my loyalty extends to your mate as well. I'd give my life for both of you, and not just because he carries a part of your soul."

"I know. He's a better man than either of us. Speaking of help, though, you could start by going to the store. I didn't have a chance to pick up more bruise cream and Bacitracin. He was hurt pretty badly."

"It's gonna take me years to look at myself in the mirror again. I'm on it. Would you uh...mind if I stay here afterwards until he wakes up? I think a little more grovelling is in order."

Lucas chuckled and felt the last of his anger being released. Bastian was a good man once you pulled his head out of his ass. "Sure. I'll see you in a bit."

Lucas returned to his seat. After closing the door, he pondered his next move. He'd come to this house first knowing that if the Mackaeo caught up to them, Bastian would be able to 'port Kyle to safety without the Order knowing. As far as anyone but he and Bastian knew, his friend was just another Tsielen who lacked power. They couldn't track him if they didn't know. It seemed that now, however, he might need Bastian to travel with them for a while. At least until he was positive they weren't being followed.

A noise stole his attention and he turned to see his mate standing timidly at the foot of the stairs. "I thought you were asleep."

"I couldn't sleep without you."

Lucas smiled and opened his arms. "Come here." Kyle curled up in his lap, rubbing his face along the column of Lucas' neck. "How are you feeling?"

"Better, Sir. Are you and Bastian...?"

"We're fine. He wants to speak with you when he gets back. Is that okay?"

Kyle nodded. Lucas revelled in the way his mate's slender body fit so perfectly against his and felt himself harden against the soft mounds of the man's ass. Talking about the ordeal Kyle suffered at the hands of Craig had refreshed the desperation he'd known in those long hours of having to wait until Kyle woke up. Of having to feel his pain through their bond until his mate was finally able to give him the location of the cabin. He needed to assure himself that Kyle was here with him and safe.

Lowering his mate gently to the floor, he grazed his lips across Kyle's — lightly at first — then kissed him passionately. Putting as much tenderness as he could into the strokes of his tongue, he made his way down the crease in between Kyle's ear and Adam's apple. Inhaling deeply, the scent of his mate permeated his lungs, intoxicating him. The lithe form shivered beneath him as he licked along the throbbing pulse in Kyle's neck down to the dip between his clavicle bones.

Lucas brought his lips back up to Kyle's mouth and began drawing in each panting breath, sweeping his tongue over the luscious curve of those red lips and nibbling on them hard enough to earn several ragged gasps. He brushed his fingertips underneath the hem of Kyle's shirt and along the defined ridges of his abs, relishing the feel of firm muscle beneath the softest flesh he'd ever had the pleasure of touching. A guttural moan was drawn from him as his mate's slender pelvis lifted and rolled seductively against his own. The friction of their cocks rubbing together sent bursts of colour blazing behind his eyelids.

It was the most sensuous feeling in the world. Never had he felt more in control, yet sensitive to the every movement of the pliant, welcoming body under his. He wanted to take his time exploring the gentle curves and hidden caverns of Kyle's body—to caress his tongue across every inch of pale skin—but the sensations were too much for his patience.

Unable to wait any longer, Lucas quickly removed the offending material between them. Shirts were ripped away and he reminded himself at the last second to ease Kyle's pants off with care. Grabbing a pillow from the couch, he lifted his mate's behind then slid the cushion underneath.

Leaning his much larger frame over Kyle, he grasped both of their cocks in one hand and stroked them together in long, demanding pulls. With each pass of his palm across their engorged heads, he gathered clear pearls of pre-cum and used them for lubrication. He created a fierce rhythm that had them both shuddering with such ferocity that when their lips came together, they mashed with frantic intensity.

"Please, S-sir. I need you in me. Please!"

The begging and provocative whimpers coming from deep within Kyle's throat escalated Lucas' arousal until the drive to possess him became too much to control. "Don't move," he said roughly. He snatched a bottle of lube out of the drawer in the coffee table and slicked his fingers.

Kyle laughed brightly and smirked at him. "Always prepared, huh?"

"With you I have to be. You drive me insane."

His mate's next laugh ended in a sharp hiss as he eased one finger deep into Kyle's tight hole. Bending down to suck and bite at the man's hardened nipples, he stretched Kyle as fast as he could. Pants soon turned to loud cries as he pegged Kyle's prostate over and over again.

Lucas removed his fingers once he was satisfied and lifted his mate's ankles to rest on his shoulders. After lining up his cock with Kyle's quivering hole, he slammed himself in, grunting with the overpowering feel of muscles clenching his swollen member. Kyle's lashes grew damp and Lucas searched his emotions for any sign of distress, but there was only excitement and need. Growling, he pounded into Kyle's sheath, feeling the pain of his rough entrance mix with pleasure in his mate.

Still he needed more. The memory of the haunted look in Kyle's eyes earlier, his refusal to respond through their link, sparked an undeniable urge to reassert his dominance—to dispel any lingering doubts in his mate's mind that he was cherished, claimed by the one man who understood just how precious he was.

Lucas stopped his thrusts, his cock pulsing with the need to conquer the demands of the constricting channel that gripped it. *Look at me.* Kyle's head ceased its thrashing and eyes dazed with turbulent lust met his. *Do *not deny me again. You are mine.*" Each word was punctuated by a deep, hard lunge that enforced his command, yet his emotions portrayed the yearning desire he had for his mate to accept his authority of his own volition.

The supple body beneath his quivered and Kyle wrapped his small hands around his wrists. Kyle angled his pelvis higher and added his own strength to the slow, merciless pummelling. "*Never again, Master.*" The feel of Kyle's willingness to surrender everything charged through Lucas in an empowering rush. Increasing the speed of his strokes, he let loose his inhibitions and took what was his.

When Kyle arched his back suddenly, Lucas knew he was close to coming but unable to warn him. "Come, boy. Now!" With a shout, Kyle climaxed and spurted ribbons of cum across his chest. Lucas came seconds later, filling the man's battered channel with streams of warm semen. The bliss on his mate's face was enough to rob him of what little air remained in his lungs.

A loud harrumph coming from somewhere in the kitchen brought both men back to awareness.

"You know, as appealing as the scenery is from your kitchen window, I think I'd much prefer to be doing unspeakable things with someone in my own living room, thank you very much. So whenever y'all are done in there…" Bastian called out with more than a little hint in his voice.

Lucas cursed and leaned over to kiss the blush rising in his mate's cheeks. He used the remains of his shirt to wipe the cum from Kyle's chest, then wrapped him up in the blanket from the couch before Bastian made an appearance.

"Go on up to the bedroom and dress, then come down and join us." When he'd made sure Kyle was out of sight, he yanked his pants on and called out to his friend to let him know it was safe to come back in.

Bastian, a smartass who never disappointed, started off with, "You know, if y'all wanna get really kinky, I got a vidcam in the back seat of my car that hasn't seen any action since I was with that hot little…"

"TMI…"

"Just saying. Y'all were gettin' pretty frisky with the…"

"One more word, Bastian…"

"Damn, you're grumpy after you get a piece of…"

A pillow sailed across the room and smacked Bastian in the head, ending his sexual tirade. "Ouch!"

"Serves you right. Your timing stinks." Lucas didn't miss the bulge in his friend's pants as he walked over and handed him the bag of medicine. "Thanks man. Listen, I was thinking about where Kyle and I will go from here. My original emergency plans will work for the most part. I have enough alternate identities and properties to lose them within a matter of months, but I never planned on having a mate with me. I was wondering…"

"Way ahead of you, man. I put in for a leave of absence at work while I was out. Soon as I beg your lovely mate for forgiveness, I'll go pack my bags. Just let me know whenever you want to leave."

Grinning widely, Lucas clapped his friend on the shoulder. "I'll owe you for this."

"No," Bastian said, the humour fading from his expression. "All my life you've been protecting me. This is my chance to return the favour. Whether it takes a few months or a century, I'm with you. Feel me?"

"Yeah. Now go grab some beers before I get all teary-eyed."

Bastian laughed and shook his head as he walked into the kitchen.

Chapter Nine

"Take the pillow."

"I don't need it anymore. I feel fine."

"Quit trying to top from the bottom and do as I say."

"Top from the...what?"

Bastian hardened his eyes. "Disobey me. Now take your pillow."

"But the bruises are almost gone."

"Really."

The man moved with blurring speed, spinning him around by the arm and smacking him solidly on the ass. Kyle yelped in pain and cupped his sore bottom with both hands.

"Something tells me you're going to need a little cushioning for the additional bruises from last night."

The glare he shot Bastian might have been more intimidating were his face not flaming with embarrassment. He had finally convinced Lucas that he was ready, physically and emotionally, for the spanking he'd always desired from the man. It had been wonderful, completely erotic, and *private!* Thinking of it now caused his cock to swell, drawing Bastian's eyes to the obvious tent in his pants.

"I can feel you getting irritated. Behave."

"Ugh!" Kyle flung his hands into the air and stomped to the room to grab his pillow, ignoring Bastian's snicker. He had only himself to blame. Instead of letting the man suffer, he'd offered forgiveness, and since then had been living under the rule of two aggressively protective Doms. One he was bonded to, and one who was like the second older brother he'd recently discovered he'd never wanted.

"Behave or I'll have to tell Deluc a punishment is in order."

Kyle stopped on his way back to the foyer. "You wouldn't." Though his punishments never involved pain, consuming remorse was inevitable. The knowledge that he had failed Lucas in any way was a punishment all on its own.

"If I recall correctly, your last punishment was followed by a reward that I have no doubt you enjoyed." Bastian frowned as another thought seemed to come to him. "I'm going to have to remind Deluc that he's supposed to resist temptation during a punishment. Though I can't blame him. Sexy as you are, I think I'd forget myself."

Snorting, Kyle opened the front door and walked to the car. Though their relationship was strictly platonic, Bastian took every opportunity to compliment his looks, his apparent submissive grace, and everything he did to please his Master. Kyle still couldn't figure out why but apparently not only did Bastian thoroughly enjoy doing so, but Lucas encouraged his friend. Kyle treasured each compliment as much as he did his lover's praise.

That confession, however, would never pass his lips.

They drove to a small café Lucas would meet them at when he finished shopping for supplies. The name of the town escaped Kyle. Two weeks of travelling from state to state had leached the distinctions between the many different cities and suburbs. Not that it mattered. Every night was spent under the loving yet firm control of his Master, every day filled with security.

Life just didn't get any better.

"We'll be leaving again in the morning. I've got a cabin up in Michigan that'll be nice to visit for a few days or so. Ever been?"

Unwelcome memories of the last time he'd been in a cabin popped into Kyle's mind. Craig leering, toys used as torture devices spread out behind the man on the workbench. Craig's voice spouting a myriad of insults and threats. Unbelievable pain fragmenting his mind until nothing else existed.

"Kyle?"

He could still feel the steel bands cutting into his wrists. Skin stretched taut from the pull of his suspended, naked body. Rivulets of sweat mixing with the tears that streamed down his face.

"Kyle!"

So caught up was he in the terror of his memory that he failed to register the car coming to a stop, or the sound of his seatbelt buckle being unlatched. Kyle felt an arm snake around his waist and he reared back. Two large hands braced the sides of his head, tilting it back so that he had no choice but to meet a set of stern, brown eyes.

"Breathe."

The command was low, inflectionless and utterly compelling. His throat opened and sucked air in.

Recognition of his surroundings followed and Kyle lifted a shaky hand to Bastian's chest. Instantly, he was pulled against it and held tightly. Convulsive shudders racked his body and his chest heaved with dry sobs but he refused to shed a tear. Never again for the monster who had ripped away his manhood.

Bastian fished for the vibrating phone in his pocket and perched it between his ear and shoulder, leaving his arms free to keep Kyle trapped against him in a solid embrace.

"He's right here. No, he's all right, just a little shook up. I think he had a flashback. I mentioned visiting my cabin and he freaked out." There was a long pause, then, "Fucking hell. All right, I've got this." After a few seconds, Bastian's tone became exasperated. "Dude, I know he's your mate but I love the little guy, too. Stay there and have some faith in me. I'll take care of this."

The cell phone hit the floor a moment before a kiss was pressed into Kyle's hair. When Bastian's last words finally sank in, his fear was replaced with confusion. *Did he really say…?*

"You love me?"

The band of arms around him loosened enough for Kyle to peer up at the man. Their faces were mere inches apart but it wasn't uncomfortable. Sincerity and…yes, it was love, shone down on him.

"Of course. Don't get me wrong. I mean, Deluc's great and all but I find you much easier on the eyes." The suggestive wriggle of his brows elicited a sharp burst of laughter from Kyle. "That's what I wanted to hear. Do that at least twenty more times today and you'll make me a happy man."

"That was quick. Wait, is he flirting with you again?"

"Tell your mate he owes me big for doubting my skills." Bastian let go to interlace his fingers and stretch them forwards to pop his knuckles, flexing his muscles in a boastful manner. "He may be your Master, but I am *the* Master."

Kyle rolled his eyes. It was impossible to dwell on the misery of his former life while in the company of his Doms. *His Doms.* The thought was unbidden yet true. For all of his faults and arrogance, Bastian had somehow come to be an integral part of his life.

"When it's safe, can we move back to the first house we went to?"

"Well that answers my question. Tell him I said that's cheating. And yes, we can live there to stay close to Bastian."

"Thank you, Sir." His happiness was reflected in the current of approving contentment Lucas sent back. A thought occurred to him and it was blurted out before he could stop himself. "Do you think Lucas loves me?"

Bastian subdued his levity and laid a reassuring hand on his knee. "Sweet cheeks, I'd bet my left nut that the man fell in love with you the day he met you. I know I would have. Granted, he was the last person I expected to find a soul mate, but a bond cannot be made in the absence of love. So I guess the real question is…why haven't you told Deluc you love him?"

Kyle ducked his head to hide his blush behind the locks of his hair. There wasn't an answer for that other than cowardice. It was still hard to believe sometimes that he was truly wanted despite all of his hang-ups.

"Well, let's go in and grab a bite to eat. I'm starving." Bastian picked up his cell phone from the floorboards, exited the car then waited for Kyle to join him. Keeping a territorial hand on Kyle's elbow, he walked to a booth towards the back of the diner where they sat down across from each other, Kyle on his pillow. The man's possessive nature in the absence of Lucas' presence had long ago ceased to bother Kyle. He had a feeling his submissiveness brought out the dominant in Bastian that only served to strengthen his sense of security.

A cute brunette with a high ponytail and red-rimmed glasses bounced over to take their orders. As expected, Bastian ordered for both of them then turned on the charm. In no time, the girl was giggling and touching the man at every joke and flattering comment he threw out. When she at last walked away, Bastian sat back with a smug grin.

"What?"

Kyle shook his head. "You have a compulsive flirting disorder, don't you?"

"Hey, not all of us can get as lucky as Jonathan and find the perfect sub and partner. Until I do, I gotta make the most out of what there is."

Jonathan. It was Lucas' new public identity. Kyle had also been given a different name but had trouble remembering to respond to it around others. Instead of yelling at him for it, though, both men simply addressed him by different terms. Bastian's favourite was 'boy' and Lucas stuck to his usual 'sweetness'.

When their food arrived, Kyle entertained himself between bites by listening to the man's cheesy seduction and watching the girl fall head over heels for it. Bastian's knack for detecting the willing and available really was amazing. Male or female, young or old, they were attracted to him like moths to a flame. Kyle had yet to see the man get any real action, though. It was too dangerous to let anyone know of their whereabouts.

Eventually the girl left and Kyle asked, "If you can't sleep with them, why do you still flirt?"

"Keeps my skills sharp. Plus it gives me a face to picture at night when I listen to you guys going at it."

He screwed his face up disgustedly. "You're one sick puppy, you know that?"

Bastian grinned wickedly. "And you're one loud little spitfire. How am I supposed to ignore the delightful sounds you make?"

Kyle felt his entire body heat as he gaped in disbelief. "I'm not that loud."

"Yes you are, but don't curb your enthusiasm on my account. It's the next best thing to having a warm body in my bed to play with."

It was impossible to tell whether he was serious or not but Kyle didn't think he wanted to know. Thankfully, the rest of their conversation consisted of talk that revolved around subjects other than sex, for which he was profoundly grateful. By the end of the meal—like clockwork—the waitress had slipped a folded piece of paper under the bill and told Bastian when her shift would be over. Kyle was surprised it fit in the man's pocket what with the numerous other numbers he'd stuffed in it during the past few weeks.

"Stay here while I pay the bill."

"Yes, Sir."

Lucas should be joining them at any minute. An unexpected sickening feeling entered the pit of his stomach and he lurched forwards as a surge of anger tore through him.

"Tell Bastian to 'port you. Get out of there now!"

Kyle looked up frantically and saw a huge man move to stand a little too close to Bastian at the register. Just as he slid out of the booth, he was yanked against the unyielding length of another large man. Something sharp pierced the skin on his side and he bit his tongue to keep from crying out.

"We're going to walk out of here nice and easy," the stranger said in a hushed, cold tone. "If you try to run, it'll be the last thing you do."

His frightened gaze met the rage blazing out of Bastian's eyes a moment before they were both herded out of the café. In the parking lot, three men flanked Bastian, detaining him while his own captor prodded him with a blade towards a black sedan.

"They have us. Lucas, they have Bastian."

"Shit! Don't let him 'port in front of them. They can't find out about him."

At that moment, Bastian elbowed one man in the gut and swung a fist at another. He fought wildly then made a break for Kyle as soon as he saw an opening.

"Bastian, no!" The knife jabbed deeper and Kyle was shoved roughly into the backseat of the car. The man was on him at once, pressing the blade into his throat.

"Drive."

The car jerked and spun as the driver slammed on the gas. Kyle remained still until he saw his captor take a syringe from a side compartment and aim it at his arm. He kicked out and shoved but his struggles were useless. The man pinned him easily beneath his hulking weight and jammed the needle in.

"Master!"

Kyle was out before he got an answer.

* * * *

Lucas eyed the group of traitorous Mackaeo that had caught him by surprise, encircling him at the edge of the parking lot of the grocery store he'd just come from, then glared at his former commander. The man was still built like a brick—square angles and overdeveloped muscles with a scalp as smooth as marble. Connor smiled in satisfaction at whatever message he'd just received on his phone then raised his steely gaze. "Before we go any further, I want you to take a look at something."

Holding the phone face out, he stepped forwards just enough for Lucas to make out the picture on it. His recognition of the reddish-blond hair and delicate features was immediate. Kyle's face was slack in unconsciousness but blessedly free of any marks. Even though the break in their connection had alerted him to Kyle's current condition, knowing his mate was in the hands of the treacherous group of Mackaeo brought his temper to a boiling point.

"If you hurt him in any way, I will kill you and your men."

"My men? They used to be yours, too. Whatever ever happened to comradeship among your fellow Mackaeo?"

"You gave up the right to call yourself Mackaeo the moment you went against the Queen's orders and started killing humans for profit."

Connor kept his expression neutral while he gestured with one hand for his men to lower their weapons. Lucas felt the dampening effect one of the guys had held on his power lift, but it was no consolation. So long as they kept Kyle unconscious in an unknown location, there was nothing he could do.

"Let's continue this conversation on our way to the compound, shall we?" Turning his back to Lucas with confidence, he opened the back door of a nearby car and waved his hand for Lucas to precede him. The others climbed into their own vehicles and formed a line as they made their way onto the interstate.

"How did you know?" Lucas asked, not bothering to hide his contempt.

"Your employees were more than cooperative in giving me information. I found it a little too coincidental that you used your power then disappeared at the same time the human who was living with you did. It doesn't match your MO of solitude to take a plaything with you into hiding. Naturally, I deduced that you had bonded with him. It was appalling to find you had lowered yourself to mate with a human, but after seeing him, I can't say I blame you."

"How did you find us?"

"We've been keeping tabs on Bastian for years. It took us a while to locate him. He's not exactly sociable with his own kind, but after that I knew it was only a matter of time before you contacted him again. Don't worry. He's of no use to us. My men have already informed him that if he gets any bright ideas like running to the Queen or attempting a suicide rescue, your life will be forfeit. Other than that, he's free to do whatever he wants."

"And what about my mate?"

Connor fixed him with a vacant, black stare. "That depends on you. I can offer the same proposal for him as I did for Bastian. If you work for me, I'll see that he spends the rest of his years living comfortably and financially stable — under supervision, of course."

Lucas' suspicions rose. The ability for mates to speak telepathically with each other was common knowledge to his people. The only way to keep him from talking to Kyle and finding him was if his mate remained in an unconscious state. "What are you not telling me, Connor?"

With a malicious twist of his lips, the commander replied, "Oh that's right. You haven't been around to hear about our latest breakthrough. You remember Sereck, right?" He didn't wait for an answer. "He developed this wonderful drug that inhibits certain receptors in the brain, effectively cutting off the ability to receive messages sent telepathically. There is no lasting damage as far as we know, but I'm afraid you two won't be communicating with each other again.

"The injections need to be administered bi-weekly, but I think we can wait for yours until we get to the compound. The dose we gave your little toy was laced with a powerful sedative. He'll be out for hours."

Clenching his fists, Lucas turned his gaze out onto the flat land passing by. One swift hit with the heel of his hand would end Connor's miserable life and give him a hell of a lot of pleasure, but he stifled the urge. "He is my mate and you will refer to him as such."

"Fine. I'll keep my men from your pretty little *mate* if you agree to come on board."

"I want him put up in a house and given a monthly allowance that will support him no matter what he wants to do with it. I also want real-time video recordings of him every week. His privacy is not to be disturbed, however. Install the camera in a fitting location and access it via remote control so that I can see that he is unharmed. One bruise or scar on him and the deal is off. Your health depends on his."

Connor leant back to put more distance between them even as his chest puffed up in triumph. Lucas let him have it. Bastian was still free and his power undiscovered. It would take his friend some time to find Kyle, but he had no doubt that Bastian wouldn't stop until his mate was safely in his care again. The only decision to make was whether or not he should join them after their escape. Both men would run with him regardless of how long it took to shake the Mackaeo, but if they were caught again, Kyle and Bastian would suffer far worse than they were now.

No. He couldn't leave. The risk was too great. Tsielen bonded for life, but that didn't make Kyle incapable of loving others. Lucas would rather he find happiness under the protection of Bastian than take that slim chance that he become a prisoner for the remainder of his days.

* * * *

Several hours later, he could make out the lights of the compound in the empty darkness of the desert night. Instead of the main entrance, the driver took them in through the back.

"Not going to gloat about your victory in retrieving a deserter?"

Connor flicked him an annoyed glance. "No one leaves the Mackaeo. You died days after you left. Killed in action by a rogue Tsielen."

"So only you and your men know I'm alive?"

"Yes. I'll not be made a fool of."

All this time he thought he'd been chased by the entire Order. Disclaiming Connor's false report by somehow making others aware of his existence was a fleeting idea and quashed as quickly as it came. It would only make things worse. If he weren't placed in custody and executed for renouncing the vows he took to protect his race, he would be reinstated into the Order and essentially returned to his former life.

As for exposing Connor and his band for the lying thieves they were, it would be his word against the head commander of the Mackaeo. He had no proof. Had he accepted Connor's initial invitation to join his group and gathered evidence, participation would have been necessary. Thus his crimes would have been no less punishable than that of the others. Extenuating circumstances did not exist among the rules of the Order. Kyle would still be denied contact with him owing to the law prohibiting members of the Mackaeo to take a mate, and the relative freedom Connor was proposing for his mate would be forfeit.

Once in the main garage, they took the outer elevator directly down to the first floor below ground level. There were three floors underground consisting of the weapons rooms, training facilities, and storage and holding cells for those criminals waiting for transport and sentencing. Above ground lay the separate living apartments for each Mackaeo, spread out in a circular pattern with a larger building in the middle where they could congregate for meetings and social gatherings.

Connor and the driver walked him down a long enclosed corridor containing several doors leading to the holding cells and unlocked one on the far end. Inside was a standard sized cot and other basic amenities.

"These living arrangements won't last long. During the past few months we've been sizing down each compound and putting up others. Spreading our ranks to cover more of this country and others. In about a week, you'll be assigned an apartment with Rodego."

"How kind of you. So I'm assuming that this compound will be run solely by you and your men?"

"Yes. It should make your life and our operations run more smoothly, don't you think? I'm not a completely unreasonable man. You're not a prisoner here, merely a comrade who will remain under close supervision for the duration of your stay."

"You mean for the rest of my life."

Connor shrugged nonchalantly. "Someone will be in shortly with your injection and some food. Make yourself comfortable. I'll have a file sent to you on your upcoming assignment."

They left him alone, locking the door from the outside. Shortly afterwards, a man came in with a tray of food and a needle containing the serum that would temporarily sever the mental link between him and his mate. Gritting his teeth, he forced himself to submit to the injection and refrained from ripping the man's throat out.

Lucas spent the rest of the night exercising. It helped him to focus, but every alternative for his situation or plan of escape ended with there being too much risk to Kyle. The only thing that would bring him peace would be the knowledge that Bastian had managed to find his mate and ensure that he was happy. Unfortunately, Connor would never let him know if it happened. It would diminish too much of his control over Lucas.

Chapter Ten

Kyle awoke to the jostling of a hard body pressed tightly against his. Firm muscles flexed along his flesh underneath his layer of clothing as body heat warmed his chilled skin. *It had all been a dream.* The men. Lucas' panicked warning. Bastian fighting to get to him. All of it. He wasn't sure which of his Doms was carrying him now, but the presence of either one was strong enough to drive his fears away.

Snuggling in, he inhaled deeply and immediately tensed. The scent was wrong, as was the pressure of the fingers on his arm and thigh holding him in place and bordering on painful. The low chuckle that drifted to his ears sent a fissure of alarm racing down his spine. Opening his eyes, he peered up into a face that didn't even slightly resemble those of his Doms.

Not a dream.

Kyle shoved at the man's chest and bucked his legs out. His sudden action gained him a few seconds to roll out of

the large arms and land clumsily on his feet but a hand
clenched his hair and wrenched him back. An arm banded
around his arms and chest, constricting his airflow and
lifting him from the ground.

"Don't bruise him. We need him ready for auction by the
end of the week."

Flinging his legs wildly, he felt a sliver of satisfaction
when his right foot connected with something solid
followed by a curse. When his eyes flew open again, it was
just in time to see a fist hook towards his stomach.
Engulfing pain radiated from his gut but his body was
denied the involuntary reflex to curl in on itself. More
hands snatched his ankles and stretched out his tender abs
between two men. Still he continued to struggle.

"This one's a fighter. It'll lower his value." The voice
came from the man crushing him.

Another off to his side replied, "After the auction, I'll
teach him his place. It'll take us at least two weeks to
deliver him to his new owner. He should be healed up by
then."

Unmitigated terror leapt into his heart and he doubled
his efforts but they were in vain. A heavy iron door was
opened leading to a small, windowless room made
entirely of cement with a floor drain in the centre. The two
men holding him flung him inside where he landed
roughly on the ground, rolling several feet with his
momentum.

"Strip."

Kyle rose shakily to his feet and glowered at the pair
blocking the doorway. They parted to admit a third, who
stood taller than them by at least five inches, with a bald
head and square body. His eyes appeared black in the dim
light of the overhead, caged bulb and his face

expressionless. He nodded to the others, who began to advance on Kyle. He was outnumbered, outmuscled and definitely not dealing with his own species, but still he had to fight.

His swing at the first man was easily dodged and a vicious punch to the back of his head sent him reeling into the second. They had him stripped of every article of clothing before he could manage to look up again. Through blurred vision, he saw that all three were once more at the door. One held a thick hose with its large nozzle pointed directly at him.

Kyle scrambled until his back hit the wall but there was nowhere to run. The man flipped the latch on top and an explosive current of water shot out. It hit his face before he could react, burning his eyes and blasting down his throat in a choking torrent. The force kept him braced against the wall like a magnet and it took all of his strength to twist to the side to shelter his face and crotch. Thousands of sharp, icy needles stabbed him mercilessly. The freezing barrage numbed his skin instantly but the biting pain—like knives cutting every inch of him—remained.

The stream switched angles and drove him up from his crouched position. Just as he was about the move to his other side, it hit his cock and he screamed in agony. Kyle lost track of time. The slicing pain and aching numbness sapped every ounce of energy from him until he was reduced to a quaking mass of sodden flesh and bones.

The pounding flow ended abruptly. Hands jerked him in different directions as another set of clothes was tugged over his naked body. The movements cleared his ears of water and he was able to make out parts of the conversation going on around him.

"…see the scars on his back? Do you think Deluc…"

"...obviously he was a slave once, he will be again..."

"...find a buyer who enjoys the harsh stuff. We'll still get a decent cut. He's got the looks..."

Kyle felt himself being hoisted over the shoulder of one of the men. They were walking again and the action caused the shoulder blade to jut into his tender stomach. It wasn't long before he was tossed onto another hard cement floor with the sound of a door slamming shut ringing in his ears. In misery he lay there, rattling with convulsive shivers and lacking the strength to draw his arms and legs in close. A moan escaped at the feel of a gentle touch to his side.

"It's okay. I won't hurt you."

The tone was high-pitched and soothing, that of a young woman. She brushed her fingers through his soaked bangs and lifted them. Cracking his lids open over what felt like layers of sand, he made out the form of a small yet voluptuous woman hunched over him.

"Are you hurt anywhere?"

When his frozen lips refused to shape a reply, she called out to someone and slowly raised him into a sitting position. A man appeared, perhaps a few years older than him, and hooked Kyle's left arm over his shoulders while the woman took his right. Too weak to protest, he was led to the back of the room where more men and women sat huddled together for warmth.

After laying him down on a threadbare blanket, the woman spooned him from behind while the man tucked another, slightly thicker covering over them. He was dimly surprised to find the woman taller than he'd first guessed. Her chin rested just above the crown of his head and her long limbs draped over his.

Then the pain of heat set in. The piercing sting of needles returned and set fire to his skin and extremities. Humiliation flooded him as whimpers he couldn't suppress escaped from his raw throat, attesting to his weakness, but the woman merely held him closer.

"Shhh. Give it a minute. You'll feel better. Just try to relax."

The pain gradually eased and with it the last of his reserves. "*Lucas?*" There was no response. It felt as though a wide chasm had replaced what had once been the vibrant thread of their connection. Not even the ever-present thrum of his lover's emotions was discernible. He wanted to rip away and demand to know where his Master was but exhaustion took his will and pulled him under. He fell asleep to the quiet whispers of the woman and man beside him.

Sometime later, a loud booming noise jerked him awake and he sat up in time to see the same two men who had manhandled him throw a young man into the room. The woman beside him launched herself at the huddled form that shied away from her touch. Eyes blazing with fury, she stood and looked defiantly at the bald-headed man Kyle could now see standing behind what must be his guards.

"What are you doing to him?" she spat out.

The two burly men parted to allow Baldy through. "Nothing he can't put an end to. He knows what's expected of him, and he knows what will keep happening if he doesn't start cooperating."

Those words incited dread such as he hadn't known since Craig. The woman, however, was undeterred.

"You sick bastards! You'll kill him if you keep this up."

"I don't get paid to deliver corpses, but I will take away his eating privileges if you don't shut up right now. I will not be ridiculed by a human." Baldy paused to give her a chance to defy him but she wisely bit her tongue. "Good girl." He left with the guards trailing behind him.

The woman unleashed her fury as soon as the lock clicked into place. Flinging herself against the door, she pounded and shouted a string of invectives that would have made a stone-cold biker blush. When her futile tirade finally came to an end, she turned to the boy still huddled on the ground and made her way cautiously over to him.

"Jules…"

The man cast a baleful glance at her then clambered stiffly to his feet. His knees gave out almost immediately but when the woman moved to help, he shrugged her off. On all fours, he crawled to one side of the room, away from everyone else, and sat hunched to the side, taking care to keep his back from touching the wall. The older man who had aided Kyle earlier came up behind the woman and put a placating hand on her shoulder.

"He'll talk when he's ready, Amy. Give him some time."

"We don't have time. They're going to sell us soon and we'll probably never see each other again." In a voice drenched with unshed tears, she begged, "Jules, please. Don't shut me out."

When there was no response, she sighed and let her friend guide her back to the group. Kyle caught the flash of longing Jules sent to the retreating pair between the locks of dirty pale hair shrouding his face. He knew that look of defeated hope. That awkwardly angled posture meant to reduce pain along the backside. Kyle saw himself in every rigid line of the young man's body. There was no mistaking the tenuous mask Jules used to hide the torment of his abuse.

How many times had he blown off Lucas' concern during his employment with the man in resentment and frustration? It was a defence mechanism that he'd hated but one that had been necessary to keep from crumbling under the strain of despair.

Amy took the blanket they'd been using and laid it at Jules' feet without a word. Kyle found himself fixed by a scrutinising stare as Amy sat in front of him. Underneath the film of grime on her face and hands, she really was a beautiful young woman. Her long, raven-coloured hair curled around a pixie face that was luminescent in comparison. Despite her callous demeanour, large doe eyes and a heart-shaped mouth made it hard not to trust her.

"Feeling better?" At Kyle's nod, she asked, "What's your name?"

"Kyle."

"I'm Amy. This is Todd," she gestured to the man who had helped him earlier then went down the list of names for the seven other people occupying the room. "And that there is Jules. He's not big into talking anymore but he's a good guy. So how did they catch you?"

Kyle hesitated on his answer. She deserved the truth from him, but he didn't think now was the best time to admit that he was bonded to a man who belonged to the same species as the ones who were holding them captive.

"They took my Master. I was out with a friend when they caught us, too."

"Your Master?"

He allowed the love and pride for his mate to replace the anguish over their lost connection. Lucas was too valuable to the Mackaeo for them to kill. Though their bond was somehow broken, Kyle refused to entertain the idea that it was permanent.

"My Dom," he said, smiling.

Amy's lips formed a perfect O but she didn't comment on it further. "Jules and I met each other on the streets about four months ago. I agreed to teach him how to break into houses and cars for money." She laughed half-heartedly. "He wasn't any good at it but we were a great team. Jules could sell a dream vacation to a dying man so he met with the buyers and I stole the loot."

Her voice quieted with her next words. "They grabbed me one night when I was lifting the radio out of a Beemer. Jules was out of sight at the end of the block keeping a lookout. They were so strong I knew I didn't have a chance. I screamed at Jules to run but he's as stubborn as I am. He wouldn't leave me. We were the first to arrive here three weeks ago. Funny thing is...they were after me but this whole time they've been more interested in him." The three of them glanced at the lone figure of the beaten man.

"What do you think they want from him?"

"I don't know. He hasn't spoken a word since the first time they dragged him out of this room."

A shiver raised the fine hairs on the back of his neck. If his experiences with Craig were anything to go on, Kyle could imagine what Jules was hiding from Amy. Sometimes it was better to protect friends from the truth when there was nothing they could do to help.

"Why did they bring you here?"

The look passed between the woman and Todd did nothing to alleviate his foreboding. "We're to be sold as slaves. They didn't tell you?"

His thoughts careened down a path he'd hoped never to travel again. It seemed a divine prank that he should be rescued from a lifetime of slavery only to be thrust back into it after finding real love. Looking at Jules, a reflection of himself as a slave to Craig's maniacal demands, he knew he couldn't survive another round.

Death, however, was not an option. If he allowed himself to waste away, he would be sacrificing not only his life, but the piece of Lucas' soul intertwined with his. They would both die for his failure to hold on until Lucas came for him. Or Bastian. Kyle's very presence here had to mean that Bastian had heeded his warning and kept his power under wraps — or they would still be on the run trying to figure out a way to break his mate free.

He had to have faith. Lucas was the most powerful man he'd ever met, and Bastian was too much of an asshole to let the Mackaeo get away with outsmarting him and taking the two men he loved. Kyle willed his terror to shrink in the face of his newfound confidence. Bastian would find him and 'port them all to safety. He was as certain of it as the love he held for both of his Doms.

His elated grin made Amy and Todd frown and scoot back as though his impulsive spark of insanity might be contagious. It wouldn't be easy to explain to them that not all Mackaeo, or Tsielen for that matter, were a threat. Looking around at the room of lost souls waiting to be sold, he knew they needed to hear that there was hope. Especially one in particular.

Leaving the pair to stare at him perplexedly, he walked over to Jules, who watched him approach warily. Kyle sat beside him a few feet away. Kyle guessed him to be around the age of eighteen or nineteen, though his small, willowy frame had made him appear younger at first. His features were soft yet gaunt, with dark bags under his light blue eyes. Limp hair hung down to his slim chest and the same flimsy rags Kyle had been dressed in revealed pale skin marred by a collection of bruises and welts, both old and new.

Still, the man was stunning. The challenging look in his eyes brought sudden clarity to Kyle. They were training Jules — just as Craig had once trained him to abandon his independence and accept his boyfriend's authoritarian rule. The fact that they concentrated on breaking Jules instead of the rest of the flock could only mean that he'd already been sold and that his new owner wanted him docile and pliant.

The thought made Kyle sick but he pushed his revulsion aside. "I was a slave once. I thought my boyfriend loved me but all he really wanted was someone to control. He took everything from me, and when that wasn't enough, he punished me for it. I knew he would kill me eventually but I couldn't escape. For five years I lived in hell until I met the man who saved me."

Ignoring Jules' scowl, he continued. "Lucas used his power to find me after my boyfriend Craig had kidnapped me. By rescuing me, he sacrificed everything in his life. He showed me that I didn't have to be afraid anymore, and I've been in love with him ever since."

"What do you mean 'his power'?"

Kyle paused, unsure of how much to divulge about their captors. Then again, if they were all sold into slavery before Bastian could find them, didn't they deserve to know the truth behind the men who had kidnapped them? Keeping his gaze on Jules, he replied, "He is Tsielen, part of the same species that kidnapped all of you. More specifically, he once belonged to the Mackaeo — a group of

Tsielen who are assigned to police their kind because they each possess a power. The same group that is holding us now."

A collective gasp swept the room and he braced himself for the rebuke he knew was coming.

"And you love him? What kind of twisted, masochistic freak are you?"

Kyle frowned. It wasn't Amy's reaction over his admission of love for a man associated with their captors that surprised him. That had been expected. It was her utter lack of a reaction to the knowledge that they were being held by nonhumans that made him hesitate. Did Connor and his men have so much confidence in their control of the slave trade that they were willing to share the secret of their people with the humans they'd stolen? Looking around at the others and seeing only revulsion on their faces instead of fear, he realised that must be the case.

"The men who are selling us make up only a portion of the Mackaeo. They're going against the laws of their people and their Queen just to make a fast buck. When they gave Lucas an ultimatum to join them or die, he ran. He couldn't bring himself to harm humans and go against the beliefs of the majority of Tsielen. It took him four years to get this renegade pack of Mackaeo off his trail. Then he gave up his quiet life of retirement just to save me. Once they detected the power he used to rescue me, they started to hunt for us."

Turning so that Jules knew that what came next was aimed at him, he said, "When Tsielen fall in love, they give a part of their souls to their lover. I hold a piece of Lucas' soul, and he holds a part of mine. We became soul mates. He did everything he could to keep me safe."

"If he loves you so much then why are you here?"

Kyle didn't let Amy's snide scepticism get to him. She had ample reason to doubt his words. "I don't know. Something went wrong, but it's because he loves me that I know we'll get out of here. All of us."

Amy snorted, though her voice took on a decidedly less derisive tone. "And just how is that supposed to happen?"

"Bastian. He's Lucas' best friend and he loves me, too. He has the ability to teleport as well but our captors don't know that. He'll be able to find me, and when he does he'll take us all away from here. You'll see." Okay, that sounded lame even to him, but the strength of his conviction sparked a glimmer of hope in the faces of the dispirited bunch around him. It was evident in their doubtful expressions. They wanted him to prove his words as much as he wanted them to believe.

It would take time, he knew. They just had to survive until then. Several minutes later, he was rewarded when Jules picked up the blanket at his feet and, fluffing it out, extended a corner in offering. Jules kept his gaze downcast but Kyle smiled his gratitude anyway. Together they sat in shared warmth and companionable silence, awaiting whatever was in store for them next.

Chapter Eleven

Time was measured by the hunger pangs in his belly. Being no stranger to starvation, he judged that they were being fed once a day. The meals consisted of an unidentifiable substance which only redeeming value lay in its tastelessness. At the second arrival of food delivered by Baldy's guards, though, they didn't leave right away as they had the last time. Instead, they passed around the bowls then marched straight for Jules.

The young man flung aside the blanket they shared and stood with his hands clenched at his sides. Kyle jumped up as well, unable to sit by while they dragged his new friend off for more torture and degradation.

"Leave him alone. He hasn't even eaten yet."

His outburst took the men by surprise for a moment. Then both guards laughed uproariously and continued their advance. As one of them reached out for Jules' trembling form, Kyle snatched at his arm but was backhanded before anyone could react. Skidding to a halt several feet away, he heard Amy's angry yell and felt fingers brush along his busted lip. Expecting to see her when he raised his lids, he was shocked to find Jules' beseeching eyes staring down at him.

"Damn it, Braman, we're supposed to leave that one's face alone."

"Then we'll buy him some makeup." Kyle opened his mouth to warn Jules when he saw the first man begin to advance on them again but his friend was faster. Jules spun around and held up his hand, stopping the guard in his tracks. That beseeching gaze met his once more. Then Jules lowered his hand at the same time as his head and walked to the door without a shred of defiance left in him.

As soon as the trio was gone, Kyle mimicked Amy's earlier actions and threw himself at the door. No one interfered as he pounded his fists and screamed at the top of his lungs. He knew it was useless. They all did, but the impotent fury inside was more than he could contain.

Jules had been the only one over the past few days to offer him comfort after his confession. While the others sent him hateful glares and viewed him as sleeping with the enemy, Jules had withheld his judgement and given silent support. What tore him up the most was the pleading look and posture of subjugation in his friend as he'd left the room. Jules had clearly not wanted Kyle to get injured on his behalf, but giving up was so much worse.

Please don't lose yourself now, he begged silently. When his voice gave out and his fists could do no more than thump dully against metal, he collapsed to the ground.

"I was wrong about you." Kyle looked over to Amy's sorrowful face. "Anyone who cares about my baby that much can't be a bad guy, no matter who he chooses to be with." At his questioning frown, she blushed and said,

"Yeah. I love him. I wanted to tell him before…but then this…" A large tear slipped down one smudged cheek. "We'll save this for him, okay?"

Glancing down to the bowl of porridge by her knees, he nodded glumly and took the hand she held out for him.

The hours passed by with interminable slowness. In pairs and threesomes, everyone held on to each other. Their unspoken relief screamed louder than the thick silence. They all hated what they knew was being done to Jules, but they all were just as grateful it wasn't them the guards took away periodically. Though he didn't feel the same, he couldn't fault them for it. None of them had done anything to deserve this and most likely none of them had ever had to face such harsh conditions.

Footsteps sounded in the hallway outside, giving Kyle and Amy seconds to move back before the door was shoved open. Jules' slack body was tossed in and the men left without a backwards glance. Amy ran to Jules but came up short when he drew away from her touch. Kyle joined them then, keeping his distance so that his friend wouldn't feel crowded. It was painful to watch him push weakly to his hands and knees only to slump to the side in a boneless heap. Swollen blue eyes fluttered closed in a face lined with pain.

As Kyle stood to retrieve a blanket, Amy gasped and several of the others screamed. Whirling around to confront the new threat, he felt every muscle in his body freeze in shock. Standing by the door, looking as cocky as ever, was Bastian—fashion statement and all. It took Kyle all of two heartbeats to break from the stupor of disbelief and pitch himself into the man's outstretched arms.

"I knew you'd come for me! I knew it. I'm so glad to see you." Kyle kissed him on the lips in his excitement, at which point Bastian simply chuckled and hugged him closer.

"Well it's nice to know that not everyone doubts me. Keep it down, little one. There's Mackaeo everywhere. Are you hurt?" Without waiting for a response, Bastian set him down and began inspecting his body for injuries.

"No, I'm fine. Got the coldest shower I've ever had in my life a few days ago but that's it." The man stared into his eyes, concern written in every feature. "Honestly, I'm good. Can we leave now before we're sold into slavery?"

"Sold into what?" The chilling note in Bastian's voice promised death and it made Kyle feel all the more secure in the man's presence.

"They plan to sell us as slaves. All of us."

Bastian took his first look around the room and cursed. When his gaze landed on Jules' beaten form, he strode over and knelt down. Amy placed herself defensively between the two men, ready to do battle despite the odds.

With a gentle tone, Bastian said, "I won't hurt him, angel. I just want to make sure he's fit for travel."

Amy cast a hard glance at Kyle. "Is this your lover?"

"No. This is Bastian. The man I was telling you would come to rescue us. You can trust him."

She hesitated but eventually moved to give Bastian access. Jules' eyes were wide and full of fright. The moment Bastian brought his large hand towards him, the frightened youth lurched away.

"Don't move." The domineering tone brooked no argument. With a skilled touch, Bastian surveyed the damage. Jules trembled and whimpered as certain parts of his body were prodded with care but otherwise made no move to back away. "All of you put a hand on me and close your eyes." When only Kyle complied, he barked, "Now."

At once the others clustered around him and timidly did as they were told. A sense of displacement passed through Kyle and the refreshing rise in temperature let him know they had made it out.

"Kyle, come with me." Bastian picked Jules up, who was now shaking violently, and headed down a long, dark corridor.

"I'm coming with you."

Pausing to give his attention to Amy, Bastian softened his tone. "I know you're concerned about him, but I need a set of impartial hands for this. Take the others and feed them. You'll find a second bathroom upstairs for anyone who wants to shower and four guest bedrooms available. Have a little patience, angel. I promise to take good care of him." With that he pivoted and beckoned Kyle to hurry.

They entered the downstairs bathroom where Kyle was ordered to lay several towels on the floor and fill the tub with lukewarm water.

"What's your name, sweetheart?"

"Jules," Kyle provided. "He hasn't talked since they captured him. Bastian, I think they were trying to train him. Like Craig trained me."

If this news bothered the man, he didn't let it show. Setting Jules down on the towels but retaining his grip, he said, "I'm going to take your clothes off now then put you in the bath." Jules shook his head furiously, trying to twist out of Bastian's grasp. "Enough. I already know what they've done. You're too weak to bathe on your own so you *will* let me help you. Understand?"

Kyle could see that his friend was doing everything to keep his tears at bay but a few rolled past his heavy lashes.

After several convulsive swallows, Jules lowered his head in consent. With exceeding caution, Bastian peeled away the offending clothes while Jules bit his lip to keep from crying out. The big man had been right. The myriad of bruises in the shapes of hands, canes and various other instruments would have sent Amy into a destructive frenzy. The only positive aspect was the absence of blood.

"Below the sink you'll find a first aid kit. I think you know what we'll need from it. Lay everything out on the counter."

"Yes, Sir." Kyle quickly followed his instructions. He heard a soft sob from Jules but resisted the urge to look until he'd completed his task. Once finished, he turned and sucked in a breath at the sight before him. The bathwater was tinted a dirty rust colour with flecks of blood swirling with every tremor that coursed through Jules' body.

"Where is all the blood coming from?" The moment the words left his mouth he wished he could take them back. He more than most should've known that not all wounds are visible on the surface.

"Hand me the spray nozzle." Bastian turned on the faucet again and pulled the plug, allowing the water to refresh itself as he rinsed Jules off. When the blood continued to leak from Jules' behind, the large man shut off the nozzle and let the tub refill. "Jules, I think you have a tear in your passage. I'll need to get some herbs for you. Do you feel safe enough to stay with Kyle for ten minutes?"

At Jules' flush of embarrassment, Kyle said, "My ex-boyfriend Craig did the same to me. Not even my mate knows about it, and I swear I'll never breathe a word of this to anyone as long as you agree to do the same for me."

He left out the part about having to go to the hospital. The absolute humiliation he'd felt at the looks of disgust on the doctors and nurses faces. The disgrace of lying so that no one blamed Craig.

Kyle thought he heard a sigh of relief from Bastian as Jules nodded. "Good. Kyle will help you finish cleaning up." Then he was gone in the blink of an eye.

"You get used to it," Kyle replied to Jules' wide-eyed look of wonder. He wanted to reassure the man that none of this was his fault. That he was safe now and they would get revenge on the Mackaeo who did this. Having been the victim, though, he knew that only time would heal Jules' wounds, inside and out. Exactly ten minutes later, Bastian reappeared and smiled down at a clean young man.

"Kyle, I put some of your clothes in my bedroom, first door on the left in the hallway. Would you mind getting something for Jules?"

Taking that as his cue to give them some privacy for Bastian to administer the herbal paste, he went out and found a pair of boxer shorts and a soft cotton T-shirt, grabbing pyjamas for himself as well. Tapping on the bathroom door lightly, he set Jules' outfit on the floor then left to check on the others. Amy had turned out to be the perfect hostess. By the time Kyle found her, she was cleaning up the kitchen after having assigned the last two people to a room.

"Let me get the dishes. I'm sure he'll want to see you when they're done."

"Is he...?" She couldn't finish her last words, couldn't even breathe.

"There was no permanent damage. He won't be dancing any time soon but he'll make it."

Amy blew out a gust of relief. "Are you sure you don't mind?"

"Nah. If my Master were here I'd be cleaning for him, and Bastian is...well, he's the next best thing."

She smiled shyly and hesitated on her way past. Kyle thought she would say something but she merely gave him a spontaneous peck on the cheek then hurried out. As much as he missed Lucas, he couldn't imagine what might have happened to Amy and Jules, or the rest of the abductees, had he not been there with them — had Bastian not loved Lucas and him enough never to give up his search.

Kyle shook those thoughts from his mind and focused on the task at hand. Once the kitchen was spotless, he crept back to Bastian's room and found his friend sitting in a recliner staring at the two small lumps in his bed. Amy lay curled around Jules in a protective embrace, much as she had with him to warm his chilled body. The comforter tucked in at their sides muffled their soft snores.

Going around to perch on the arm of the recliner, Kyle nudged the man lost in thought. "So what do you think?"

"They're beautiful."

Snorting, he elbowed Bastian in the ribs. "Not about that. About Jules. Do you think he'll be able to get through this?"

Bastian heaved a deep breath. "I don't know how Deluc did it with you. When I saw his body, I wanted to kill every single one of those bastards. I still do. I've seen a lot of shit in my day, but he's..."

"Different."

"Yeah. And the girl. She was amazing, the way she stood up to me, ready to kill for him. I don't think I've ever been so turned on in my life."

Kyle rolled his eyes but bit back the sarcastic retort on the tip of his tongue. Bastian's face held none of its usual cocky humour. The man couldn't take his gaze away from the sleeping couple. "Her name is Amy. They met on the streets not too long before they were captured. I don't think they have anywhere to go after this."

"Then they'll stay here."

Bastian was using his Dom voice as though laying down a law. While Kyle had his reservations about whether Amy and Jules would agree to this, he couldn't think of a better man to help them out until they got on their feet.

"Sir, there's something else. My bond with Lucas is broken. I can't feel him and he won't answer my calls."

At the small waver in his voice, Bastian gathered him into his lap and hugged tightly. "I'm sorry, little one. In all this chaos I forgot to tell you. I found Deluc shortly before I found you but he refused to talk to me until I made sure you were safe. As for the interference in the bond, I don't know. I'm going to go talk to him again. I'll see if he has any information on it."

The knowledge that his mate was all right brought him a measure of peace but it was a far cry from having his Master there to hold him. He could feel his heart breaking in spite of his determination to be strong.

"Has Deluc ever told you why I owe him my life?" At Kyle's shake of the head, he said, "I think I better start at the beginning then. Deluc and I have been friends since birth. At a young age all Tsielen are taught about the Mackaeo and how it's such a great privilege to develop a power and get accepted into their ranks, but we knew it was all bullshit. The average lifespan for an Order member is only one century. We learned quickly that those who thought it an honour were the ones reaping the benefits from their protection."

Bastian huffed sarcastically then bowed his head. "We were out one day playing when we discovered our powers. My father was watching from a distance and saw me teleport. He called us in to tell me how proud he was to have a son with power, but Deluc knew they would make me a killer, and I couldn't handle that at the time. He stepped forward and said he was the one my father had seen and ported in front of everyone to prove it before I could refute his claim.

"They took him from his family that day. For the longest time I couldn't live with myself. I left my family and friends and decided to join the Mackaeo like I should have done in the first place. Deluc, stubborn asshole that he is, said he would kill me if I did, and he had the skills to back it up."

Leaning back, Bastian pierced him with a determined stare. "I'm not proud of letting him take the fall for me that day, but I will get him back. I swear this to you."

His conviction was sincere. Kyle hugged him, pouring all of his appreciation into it. Movement from the bed caught their attention and they turned to see Amy holding her hand out to Bastian, who took it reverently.

"Thank you," she whispered, "for everything."

Bastian kissed her hand then lifted Kyle to stand. "Get some rest. I'll be back soon." Once the man disappeared, Kyle trudged his way to the door.

"Where are you going?" At his blank gaze, she patted the bed on the other side of Jules. "Stay. Please."

The offer warmed him and he crawled under the covers with them. The deep ache of loneliness subsided for the first time since losing his Master, and he drifted into a peaceful slumber.

* * * *

A knock on his door roused him from his musings of the thousand ways he wanted to kill Connor. Why someone would bother to knock when he was the one locked inside was beyond him, but he called out permission for entry anyway. A young Mackaeo he recognised as part of the group who had apprehended him walked in with a manila folder in one hand.

"The commander told me to give this to you. It outlines the details of our next assignment."

Damn, the commander didn't waste any time getting down to business. Lucas wouldn't be surprised if Connor had an entire backlog of missions just waiting to be carried out that only his power could facilitate. Taking the file, he threw it onto the desk and took a seat in the aluminium folding chair. When the click of the door closing didn't sound, he turned to find the man shuffling nervously from side to side.

"Is there something else?"

"Can I talk to you for one second?"

"I don't know. That's a pretty long talk."

The man grinned sheepishly, causing Lucas to appraise him with further interest. The last he knew, Connor only recruited trained killers into his little renegade group. It took a certain mindset to not only commit murder, but also go against the laws of your Queen. This man, however, displayed none of the required attributes. His trim build lacked the musculature one would accrue during assassin training and he still seemed to retain a degree of conscience that had yet to be corrupted.

"You're the one who dampened my power so that I couldn't port, weren't you?"

The man had the decency to look away in shame. "Yeah. That was me. Sorry, by the way."

Definitely not a killer.

"My name's Tailor. They told me about you. Did you really walk away from the Mackaeo?"

Lucas narrowed his eyes, noticing every jittery tic and gesture Tailor made. "Yes, I did, but only because I refused to join Connor in his illegal endeavours." Censure was implied in his tone and again the man had the grace to avoid eye contact. "What are you getting at, Tailor?"

After a full minute of opening and closing his mouth, he finally said, "If I were to help you escape, do you think you could take me with you?"

Comprehension came to Lucas and he rubbed at his temples. "He didn't give you a choice either, did he?"

Tailor shook his head. "I was only supposed to be a backup for the Mackaeo in case of emergencies. You know, if a member was chasing another rogue Mackaeo, I could dampen their power long enough for our guy to make the kill. Since that almost never happens, I was trained to investigate and file information for the Order. The commander wants me to kill humans to prove myself. If I don't, he'll kill me."

The man's voice rose with each word until Lucas had to motion for him to calm down. "I know where you're coming from, believe me I do, but I have a mate to think of as well. There is no getting out for me this time. I can't put his life in danger again."

The young man nodded, a little too enthusiastically. "Of course, of course. I'm sorry. Gotta take care of your own, right? Can't blame you, considering I'm partially at fault for you being here. I'll just, umm...I'll see you tomorrow night for the mission."

Lucas sighed heavily at the deflated hope of the man. "Wait. I might be able to do something for you. Give me some time. Once I know my mate is safe, we'll talk."

Tailor beamed at him and took his leave. Thoroughly repulsed by the new and outrageous methods Connor was using to get his dirty work done, Lucas did more exercises to vent his anger. Several hours later, a shadow appeared in the corner of his room and his heart skipped a beat.

"Is that what I think it is?"

He followed Bastian's finger to the folder on the desk. "Yeah. Plans to slaughter an entire family tomorrow night and I get to be a part of it. Didn't I tell you not to return unless you had Kyle safe with you?"

"When will you ever stop doubting me? You know, your mate had full confidence in me. Even gave me a kiss when I found him."

He couldn't speak for a full minute. "You've got him? Is he all right?"

Bastian came into the light and plopped himself down on the cot. "He misses you something fierce, but he's okay. He's at my cabin with the others."

"Others?"

His friend took on a grim expression. "When I say don't kill the messenger, you know I mean that literally, right?"

"Bastian..." he growled.

"Just making sure. I found him in a room with ten other humans. They had all been kidnapped by Connor's men and were waiting to be sold into slavery. I guess killing and pilfering wasn't enough for the bastard."

"He was going to sell my mate into slavery?" Lucas didn't even realise he had a fist reared back, ready to throw, until Bastian stepped up and got in his face.

"If you want to go at it that's fine with me, but if you want to see your mate again, I suggest you quit dicking around and help me come up with a plan."

Lucas spun and punched the wall, cracking the three-inch thick steel. "Son of a bitch! Mother fucking piece of… I'm going to kill him."

"You can't. At least not yet. If you die in the process, your mate dies with you. The main priority right now is to get you out of here."

His energy evaporated instantly and he sat down hard on the chair. "I can't leave. It's too much of a risk. If we were caught again, there's no telling what Connor would do."

"They won't catch us this time. They used me to find you, but we'll be more careful. You hid for four years."

"And I didn't have a mate to worry about at the time. You said yourself that there are ten people at your place that need your help. What would we do with them while we're on the run?" Pausing to get control of his emotions, he said, "Look, I can't keep putting Kyle's life in jeopardy. With you, he'll at least be able to live his life. I'm a ghost here without any proof of what Connor's doing. No one but he and his unit even know I'm alive. Please don't make this harder than it already is."

Bastian looked as angry as Lucas had felt when he learnt Connor's plans. Sure enough, he slammed his own fist into the wall, leaving an identical crack. "Fine. I won't argue with you but I'm not giving up, either.

Stubborn little shit.

"Before I leave, your mate would like to know why he can't communicate with you."

"Connor gave us injections of a serum that prohibits telepathic communication. Kyle's should wear off in a week and a half, but I'll still be getting them. Tell him I love him, will you?"

"No. You can tell him yourself. He's waited this long, he can wait a little longer. I'll be back to check on you." Bastian ported without another word.

Lucas leant back to stare at the ceiling. His friend was furious now but he would get over it. Eventually so would Kyle. They had to. That knowledge was the only thing that kept him from going out of his mind.

Chapter Twelve

Kyle awoke to rays of bright sunlight streaming through cream-coloured curtains. Heat surrounded him, stoking his contentedness at the feel of his lover holding him tight. Lucas' legs were intertwined with his, arms wrapped firmly around his waist as though he would never let go. His Master's semi-erect cock pressed against his, biding its time to be pleased by his mouth and hands.

It was so easy to believe.

Clear, azure eyes stared back at him when he lifted his lids. Not the deep, abiding blue of the man who dominated him only in his dreams now, but they contained a wealth of compassion that crumpled his defences and left his heart stripped bare. Jules feathered the pads of his thumbs along Kyle's spine and waited out the silent flow of his tears. They remained locked in their entangled embrace for countless minutes, each taking solace from the other until Kyle's eyes ran dry.

His gaze flicked to the large, still figure sitting in the recliner on the other side of the bed. Sometime during the night, it looked as though Bastian had aged ten years. Creases lined his forehead and his caramel eyes were circled with dark bags. The lack of his normal air of brash arrogance was appropriate, but it seemed to drive home the severity of their situation.

"I need to give Jules some more medicine. Why don't you go out and get something for you two to eat?"

Kyle looked back at his new friend who nodded his acquiescence. Disengaging himself from the cradle of too thin arms, he got up and grabbed a set of clothes for the day. After taking a shower, he ventured into the kitchen where he found Amy serving breakfast to four men of various ages — the youngest couldn't have been more than sixteen. Shivering at the thought of what might have happened to the kid if not for Bastian's interference, Kyle offered to help out.

"Thanks babe, but everything's already taken care of. Two of the girls are straightening up the rooms. The guys will be collecting firewood when they're done eating then we'll start cleaning the rest of the cabin. It's beautiful but huge. And it looks like Bastian hasn't been here in years."

Casting aside his ire at the usurpation of his role as caretaker of his Doms, he managed a wan smile. Amy — as with everyone else — was simply doing the best she possibly could under the circumstances, but it was just another reminder that his Master wasn't there to expect the same from him. He would still help, regardless, in order to keep his mind busy. Dwelling on the physical and mental rift that had come between him and his mate would only expedite the downward spiral of his turbulent emotions.

"I'm going to take a plate to Jules. I don't think Bastian wants him walking around yet." Kyle piled as much as he thought his friend could eat onto a plate. Amy stacked another plate with food and handed it to him when he was done, reminding him that he needed to remember to eat as well.

"I never did apologise for doubting you." She raised her hand at Kyle's demurral and continued. "I was jealous, really. Jules shut me out almost immediately after they took us, and it hurt that he would accept your touch and not mine. I think I know why. When I met him, he was a master at hiding the pain I knew lay just beneath the surface, but they took his mask away, and I don't think he wanted me to see what was underneath."

Taking a steadying breath, she said, "He believed in you, though. He has the most amazing knack for judging people and I should have believed in that as well. So, I'm sorry. This Bastian guy is actually pretty cool. Kinda creepy with the whole disappearing and reappearing act, but...nice. Can you take this to him?" She pulled a platter from the oven stacked with a steak, eggs, pancakes and a large pile of bacon. Kyle raised his brows at the mountain of food and she shrugged. "He's a big man. Oh, and tell him we'll need more foodstuffs soon." A smile that almost felt natural crossed his lips and he juggled the plates back to the bedroom.

Later that afternoon, when most of the men and women had retired for a nap, Kyle, Amy and Todd sought out Bastian in his study to discuss the next step. Kyle was anxious to hear news about Lucas but Bastian's persistent grimness filled him with dread.

"Is something wrong?" Kyle asked.

Rousing himself from his contemplation, Bastian cleared his throat and replied, "You could say that. Your mate won't leave. He's too afraid to take any more risks with your life."

"What?" Kyle shook his head. The words jumbled in his mind and refused to form coherent sentences. "I don't understand."

Bastian rose from his desk chair and crossed the room to him, taking his hands in a firm grip. "I've been thinking about it all night and he's right. If I were in his position, I would make the same sacrifice. I'm not saying that we call it quits, but until we can ensure that Connor can never get to you again, we have to let him call the shots on this one."

Wrenching himself away, Kyle backed up as though distance would make the problem dissolve. "So I'm just supposed to go on without him?" The sympathetic look on Bastian's face, on all their faces, was more than he could handle. "Bullshit! He's mine! I have a part of his soul. He needs me." Fire burned down his throat and through his chest but he pushed the crushing agony aside.

"Baby, the only ones who know he's alive are Connor and his men, and they won't willingly provide the proof we need to get him out. Not even the Queen knows he still exists."

Cold fury deeper than the darkest pits of hell he'd been through in his life suffused his veins. "Then I'll give her proof. Port me to the Queen."

Bastian stepped forwards with a mixture of anger and confusion contorting his face. "That's suicide. Most Tsielen aren't huge fans of humans and while the Queen has decreed that no human be harmed or killed by our people, it would still be your word against the commander of the Mackaeo."

"I'll go with you."

All three turned to the soft voice coming from the study door. Jules' pallor had a sickly cast to it and his shoulders were hunched as if it were too painful to stand up straight, but his expression held all of the boldness of a man with nothing to lose.

"He speaks," Todd said in amazement.

"Sweetheart, I can't let you…"

"I'll go too," Amy chimed in.

"And me," Todd added. "They killed my father and took me. If this is the only way to get revenge, then I'll do it."

Energised by the support of the others, Kyle quickly formulated a plan. "Tsielen may not like humans, but there's no way the Queen can ignore four of us willing to risk our lives just to tell her about Connor. If we can just convince her to conduct an unofficial investigation, we might be able to take them by surprise."

"Or she might just kill you all," Bastian ground out.

"I was a slave once, before my Master rescued me. If it hadn't been for you I would be again. I'd rather die than go through that again."

"You could die doing this!"

Kyle opened his mouth to counter his objection but stopped at Jules' cool touch on his arm. His friend limped over to Bastian and took one large hand in his.

"I know you'll get us out in time. I trust you."

Kyle knew how powerful those words were, having seen Lucas' reaction when he'd said the same. It didn't come as a shock when Bastian's adamant refusal changed to reluctance under the force of Jules' confidence.

"If we manage to get past the Queen's personal guard and she declines your request, we'll have to run from all of the Mackaeo, not just Connor and his group. Exposing yourselves will mean having to possibly spend the rest of your lives in hiding from my kind, being hunted like animals. If they find us, you could be forced to serve the Queen and her family."

"We would become her slaves?" Todd asked.

"Not as Connor would have made you but yes, you would work for her, if only to ensure that none of you divulged the secret of our kind to other humans."

"Sir, we're already on the run," Kyle pointed out. "Connor found us once before. He could do it again. I'd rather serve the Queen than become another man's slave."

Bastian let out a long, low breath, mumbling, "Deluc is going to kill me for sure this time. All right," he raised his voice to address everyone, "we'll have to go over the plan so there are no mistakes, and we'll have to do this tonight. Deluc is supposed to go on a mission and if he involves himself in any way, he could be considered a co-conspirator."

"Wait," Amy interrupted. "I think we should ask the others if they want to join us. They may have their own reasons to want to go."

Everyone nodded in solemn agreement. They filed into the living room while Amy left to retrieve the rest of the group. Though Jules wouldn't let Bastian carry him, he did consent to the request that he lay on the couch with Bastian sitting at his head.

It was clear that the youth possessed an attractive quality that went far beyond his looks, and Bastian was falling hard. Kyle's worry that Amy might feel left out dissolved when she led the others into the room and took a seat on the floor at Bastian's feet. Their bond of trust might not run as deep as the bond he shared with Lucas, but it had potential.

After explaining the risks of the proposal, only two chose to go along, for reasons similar to Todd's. The rest were homeless, just as Amy and Jules had been. Their unwillingness to become further involved was reasonable. Bastian made certain that they knew there was a choice, and he would support them no matter what their decision. The rules came next, of which there were only two — don't address the Queen directly and stay as close to Bastian as possible.

The following hours were spent in preparation in case they had to leave the cabin if the Queen refused to listen. Bastian and Amy drove into town to buy clothes, food and supplies for everyone, leaving Jules in Kyle's care. His friend had lapsed back into his silence, but there wasn't much to say. The air was tension-filled with the dangers of the upcoming event. Time crawled by for Kyle. Each tick of the clock over the mantle was like an eternity until finally Bastian decreed that they were ready.

"I've only been inside the Queen's palace twice, when I was younger, so I'm not too familiar with the layout. I do remember her throne room which is where she spends most of her time. Once I port us there, let me do the talking and try to keep in contact with me at all times."

They formed a tight circle around him and closed their eyes. The displacement lasted only a few seconds, and when Kyle opened his eyes again he felt his mouth drop open as well. The room they were now in was more like a cavernous chamber. The roof was a good twenty feet above their heads and gold leafing covered the walls in intricate, alien designs. Plush, white carpeting covered the expansive floor with tall, elegantly crafted furniture and statues placed strategically throughout the room.

A single chair, obviously the throne, dominated the far side of the room. It stood ten feet tall and looked to be made entirely of gold. The other side was taken up by two large doors also crafted with odd depictions of what appeared to be animals and Tsielen warriors.

"Damn it, she's not here," Bastian hissed.

"What is this?"

The voice wasn't particularly loud but it echoed in the vast reaches of the room. As one they turned to see two guards advancing on them from the sides of the platform the throne rested on. Each was dressed in a white and red uniform with a thick belt about the waist lined with multiple blades.

"We're here to speak with the Queen." Bastian's voice rang with command but it had little effect on the men.

"No one sees the Queen without an appointment. Guards!" The man drew a short sword from his belt as the doors to the room opened to admit three more men armed with weapons just as deadly. One pulled a knife from a scabbard strapped to his back and flung it with alarming speed. Bastian spun Jules around to shield his body then kicked the sword from the first guard's hand. It wasn't until then that Kyle saw the blade buried hilt-deep in Bastian's shoulder.

"Come to me!" Bastian shouted. Punching the second guard in the jaw, he spread his arms around as much as the group as he could and prepared to port.

"Stop!"

Everyone froze at the imperious voice that boomed throughout the chamber. Kyle couldn't move, couldn't breathe. The only thing that held him steady was the solid strength of the man he knew would protect them at all costs. Only when Bastian turned to face the newcomer could he open his eyes to look as well.

A woman as tall as Lucas with a trim yet muscular physique stood on the steps of the dais. Long auburn hair created a wavy curtain around flowing white and gold robes, and shrewd grey eyes assessed the situation with cool sagacity. It was the aura of absolute authority, however, that was her most remarkable feature.

"What goes on here?"

Bastian reached back and pulled the knife from his shoulder with only a grunt to show for his pain. Kyle didn't miss the fact that he tucked it into his belt. "We have an urgent matter to discuss with your Highness if you'll permit us to speak."

The Queen walked slowly to her throne and sat down, keeping her cutting gaze on them the whole time. At the slight dip of her head, the guards holstered their weapons and took several steps back. "You are Tsielen and therefore should know of our laws. Why did you violate them by bringing humans into my court?"

"They wanted to come as proof to the treachery of Connor, the commander of the Mackaeo, and a small group of his men. He's been murdering humans for their lands and money for years and has recently begun kidnapping humans for slaves. These humans would have been sold by him had I not rescued them."

The Queen tipped her head back and laughed. "You expect me to charge my commander with treason based on the word of humans? The Mackaeo are forbidden to have dealings with them in any form."

Her complete disregard for them angered Kyle and he found his voice. "Your Majesty?" A collective hiss sounded from the guards and he found himself pinned by the Queen's disdainful gaze.

"You had better have a good reason for speaking out of turn, little human."

Kyle thought of Lucas, of spending the rest of his life without his Master, and knew that he had all the reason in the world. "Connor kidnapped me and my mate Lu...Deluc, and threatened to kill me if Deluc didn't help him commit these crimes. My mate agreed—not because my death would mean his own, but because he would do anything to keep me safe."

The Queen pondered his words for several seconds. "I recall this Deluc. He was one of my best warriors in the Mackaeo. I was told that he died some years ago by the hand of a rogue Tsielen."

"No, Your Highness. He was given an ultimatum to either be killed or join Connor's group. He chose to run. I met him ten years after that. I owe my life to him but I came here because I love him."

"That's a telling story, young man, but I still have no proof of your accusations."

Jules stepped forward and placed a staying hand on Bastian's arm when the larger man tried to stop him. In a quiet voice that carried through the still air, he said, "Connor is bald and stands a foot taller than me. He has a scar that runs from the left side of his ribs to his navel. He can increase the density of an object to make it unbreakable but only if the object is inanimate. There's a tattoo on his back between his shoulder blades that looks like that." He pointed to an insignia on the arch of the throne just above the Queen's head.

"His second and third in command have the same tattoo in the same spot. The one that can control fire is missing part of his right ear and the other can cast illusions into unsuspecting minds."

The Queen leant forwards, her expression somewhere between annoyance and alarm. "How do you know all of this?"

"Because they did this to me." Jules took off his shirt and slowly turned in a full circle to display his front and back. The ugly bruises, welts and bite marks covering his skin stood out in stark relief against his pale complexion.

The Queen descended from her throne to take a closer look. The smaller man lowered his eyes, though whether it was in deference to the Queen or due to shame, Kyle couldn't tell. Knowing how sacred Jules' pride was to him and the humiliation he must be suffering in front of a crowd of people in order to substantiate the truth, he would guess it was the latter.

"Guards, I want a unit to take Connor into custody immediately. I want to question him myself."

"Your Majesty," Bastian interjected, "with all due respect, I would like to ask that you give me permission to apprehend Connor. It's personal to me. Once I find him, I can teleport him directly here."

Narrowing her eyes on Bastian, she nodded her head in assent. "You have twenty-four hours before I send in my guard. Mind, you must bring him in alive. Otherwise I'll have reason to doubt your honesty and will charge you with his murder. I'll call for a Mackaeo who has the ability to discern the truth before I interrogate him. These humans will be safe here until your return."

Kyle felt the breath rush from his lungs with her last sentence. His body was thrumming with excitement at the possibility of freeing his mate from the rule of a madman. To come so close and be forced to await the outcome was more torture than he could bear. Clenching Bastian's arm with both hands, he announced in the strongest voice he could muster, "I'm going with you."

Bastian pulled his forehead into a frown. "How Deluc ever got you to submit is beyond me. You're the most demanding little sub I've ever met."

Kyle flashed him a brilliant smile and held on tighter. Taking the shirt from Jules' hands, Bastian covered him again and knelt down, putting them nearly at eye level. "I'll be back for you, I promise. The Queen will make sure you're safe, okay?"

Jules studied his face for the longest time then gave him a quick kiss on the cheek. Looking more than a little satisfied, Bastian stood and cupped Amy's cheek with a smile. In the next moment, they were gone. When Kyle lifted his lids again, he cast his gaze around what looked to be a small, empty cell with sparse furniture.

"Damn it, they must have already left."

Alarm rose in his chest but he fought it down. "What do you mean they already left?"

"For the mission he was telling me about," Bastian replied grimly.

"We have to find him before he goes through with it. We've got to…" Kyle sputtered to a stop when Bastian's hand came down gently over his lips.

"What happened to the faith?" Reaching over to the desk, Bastian opened a file on top and skimmed over the details listed. "I know where this is. Let's go find your mate."

Chapter Thirteen

Connor came in with a scowl as black as a demon on its best day. He motioned for Lucas to precede him down the hall with a perfunctory jerk of his head. Knowing the reason for the expression made it hard to keep the smirk from his face.

"You look like shit."

"Shut up."

"No really, I'm impressed. For once your physical appearance matches the man you are inside."

Connor slammed him into the wall and brought his face mere inches from Lucas'. "One more word and I'll take it out of your pretty little thing's flesh."

It was an empty threat, he knew it, but that still didn't keep his anger from surfacing. Grabbing the front of Connor's shirt, he spun and smashed the man against the same wall. "Hurt him and I will end your miserable existence."

"Commander, we're ready."

Lucas didn't move an inch until Connor broke eye contact to acknowledge his second in command. This time Connor took the lead and Lucas followed them to the ground floor where they met with the young recruit, Tailor, and two other Mackaeo.

"There's been a slight change of plans," Connor said, pulling a large photograph from a manila envelope one of the men handed to him. "This is the living room I want you to port us to. Once we get there, you're to stay in this room with Tailor. Miles will bring out the kid and all you have to do is hold him while we take care of his parents. You port us back here and the job is done."

A chill raced down his spine at the implication of those words. "You want me to port the kid with us?"

"Got a problem with that?"

Lucas kept his face completely impassive as he shook his head. It had never occurred to him that Connor would want to replace the slaves he'd lost at the first opportunity. Stupid. Having Bastian risk his life a second time to port the kid out was too risky. If Connor hadn't already increased his security, it wouldn't take him long to figure out what was going on. Mind working furiously, he ported them to the chosen destination then felt Tailor's dampening power take effect.

The decorations and expanse of the living room cried wealth and prestige. It was small wonder they had waited for his particular power to do this mission. A house with this many riches laid out in such blatant display was sure to have a security system even a professional burglar would need mad skills to crack. While some members of the Mackaeo could do it, one little slip could bring the human authorities down on them in mere minutes. With his ability, they were guaranteed safe passage both in and out of the mansion.

Connor led three of his men through the foyer and up a wide staircase to the second floor. Steeling his emotions, Lucas told himself he could get through this. He had to. His only other options were few and final. If he rebelled now, he would be going up against five men, each with a power and he currently without his. Even if Tailor did decide to side with him, these men were as skilled in combat as he, making the chances of walking away very slim.

Success, however, would land him right back where he'd started, only this time Connor's men wouldn't be hunting him for his advantageous power. It would be for pride and revenge—two emotions that made for a deadly combination.

Miles returned to the room with a defiant, frightened teenager fighting and struggling against the massive arms that bound him and clamped his mouth shut every step of the way. The kid appeared to be in his late teens, with black curls flopping everywhere and a thin layer of baby fat over abs that had yet to be toned. Dressed in nothing but a pair of boxer briefs, it was plain to see where Miles' fist had landed on his stomach, probably a few times.

When the kid kicked his heel down hard on Miles' shin, the bigger man yanked him by the throat to an arm's length away and prepared to land an open-handed slap. Lucas put on a burst of speed and caught the man's wrist before it could come down.

"I'll take it from here."

Miles sneered at his deadly tone but Lucas could see the glimmer of fear in the other man's eyes. Twisting his arm free, Miles ground out, "Fine, but keep him quiet. I'm going to make sure the commander is finished."

As Miles walked away, Lucas took the kid's biceps in both hands and brought him close, meaning to calm him the way he had done with Kyle in the past, but the resemblance was too striking. Underneath the sheen of terror in the kid's eyes lay a quality of virtue he'd always imagined had once lived inside his mate long ago—before Kyle was betrayed and forced through hardships to become a monster's slave...just as this child would soon become. How many other kids would he have to sacrifice to keep his mate from the same fate?

None.

This ended now. Kyle's enduring strength lay in his ability to love and put others above himself. He had to trust in that, in the hope that Kyle would forgive him his death—for after this, it would be inevitable.

Looking deep into the kid's hazel eyes, he whispered, "I'm going to help you but I need you to stay quiet. Tailor here will look after you until I come back, okay?" When the kid didn't respond, he gave him a little shake. "Answer me, boy." That earned him a jerky nod. Leading the quaking form over to Tailor, he pushed the kid into the man's arms. "Remember what we talked about, Tailor? This is your chance. Lift your power from mine and I'll take care of the rest."

"You're going to kill them? I...I don't..."

"Tailor, they're going to make this kid into a slave. You can choose to live with that or redeem yourself. Either way, I'm doing this...with or without your help."

Tailor looked at the kid and Lucas could see the same resolution that he'd come to, cross the man's face. Lucas gave him a tight-lipped smile when he felt his power come back to life. He was glad the man was finally willing to stand behind the morals Lucas had glimpsed in him earlier, but he wouldn't ask Tailor for more. If he failed to kill the others, he didn't want Tailor to suffer the consequences should Connor find out the man had conspired with him.

"Keep him safe. I'll be right back." Porting himself to the top of the stairs, he glanced in both directions. One side of the wide corridor was encased in darkness. The other side consisted of about eight yards of balcony then stretched on to give access to a number of rooms on the left and right. Two men stepped out of one of the nearest rooms carrying a box of files and a black duffel bag. Their eyes widened and mouths opened at the sight of him.

Lucas ported directly behind them and shoved one over the balcony before he could react. The other threw the box in his face and used his power to call down a column of lightning. The heat of it singed his clothes a moment before he teleported a yard in the other direction. Now facing each other, Lucas punched the man in the temple but couldn't back away in time to avoid the arc of the knife the man pulled from his back and sliced across his chest. The man bounced back from the wall but Lucas gripped the back of his neck in one hand and the knife-wielding wrist in the other.

With brutal vigour, he smashed the man's face and wrist into the wall, which crumbled under the force. Pounding footsteps coming from the stairwell alerted him to the return of the first man and he swung the fist of the second out to the side. The blade that was still clenched in the hand of the man he held cut cleanly through the first man's throat, severing the carotid artery with precision. Lucas took advantage of the second man's shock at killing his friend and twisted his wrist, bringing the blade home deep in the thoracic cavity beneath his sternum.

Wrenching the blade free, he wiped the blood from his face in time to see Miles and Connor exiting a room several doors down. Before he could port, Miles pulled a small blow torch from his belt and lit it. Flames shot out at an impossible distance and engulfed Lucas' shirt. Searing heat enveloped him and he ported to the foyer, out of Miles' sight. Ignoring the pain, he ripped the blazing material away and stomped out the fire.

A loud crash sounded behind him and he flicked the knife blindly in that direction, grinning at the sound of a pained grunt. Another softer thump came from his right and Miles was on top of him. They toppled to the ground in a mass of limbs but the other man braced his head in both hands before Lucas could defend himself. Blinding flashes of light sparked behind his lids as his head was bashed into the floor once, twice.

Dimly he heard a shout from somewhere in the distance and one hand left his head for a brief second. Lucas brought up his knee and slammed it into Miles' groin, dazing the man long enough for him to port out from beneath him. Now at the man's back, Lucas leant down to grip his skull and chin and twisted sharply, letting go at the satisfying snap of Miles' neck breaking.

Sudden pain flared in his right breast, bringing him to his knees. A foot hooked underneath his jaw and sent him flying across the floor. Connor pounced on him before he came to a stop, driving the blade deeper into his chest The weight of the knife increased until it felt as though he'd been skewered by a three inch steel pipe.

"I should have screwed your mate while I had the chance. Guess now I'll never know how sweet it would have been."

A storm of rage surged through Lucas, igniting his blood and renewing his strength. With a guttural cry, he wrenched the knife from his chest and propelled himself forwards, twisting their bodies so that he straddled Connor's waist from above.

"Deluc, no!"

In one swift move, he flipped the blade in his hand and slammed it tip first into Connor's windpipe. "You will never have my mate," he seethed, watching with maddening rapture as the light faded from the commander's eyes.

"Master?"

Lucas jumped up and whirled around, ready to do battle with anyone else who dared get in his way. But there was no threat. Recognition was sluggish in coming, and when it did, his fury fled with the breath in his lungs. A sweep of the foyer showed him the destruction caused by his hands. Blood was everywhere, staining the floor and coating him in an obscene layer of gore.

He had never wanted his mate exposed to this side of him, the savage bloodlust that had been trained into him to cultivate the perfect assassin. This was not how it should have been. Afraid to see the revulsion and fear in Kyle's eyes, he lowered his head, the knife slipping from his numb fingers to clatter to the floor.

The pain in his body flared as a small body collided with his, pushing him back a step as thin yet powerful arms wrapped around his waist and squeezed. Stunned, he stared down at the fragile creature holding him with the ferocity of a lion.

"I love you," Kyle whispered. Raising his head so that his eyes met Lucas', he repeated in a stronger voice, "I love you. And if you ever leave me again, I'll make a trip to hell seem like paradise every day for the next eight hundred years."

A gust of laughter escaped and he fell to his knees. "You're an evil, sadistic little man."

"Damn straight." Kyle hugged his neck, nearly choking him, but nothing had ever felt better.

Reluctantly pulling away, Lucas met his mate's shimmering green eyes, seeing only love and happiness in them. "Sweetness, I'm sorry. I know I could have died and killed us both but I couldn't stand by and let him turn another innocent into a slave."

"It's okay. I would have done the same if I had huge muscles and an awesome power. I did do something but..." Kyle peered over his shoulder to the corpse behind him. "You killed Connor. We were too late. It was all for nothing."

"Maybe not yet," Bastian spoke up.

Almost at the entrance to the living room, Lucas saw his friend and the kid he'd left in Tailor's charge huddled over a motionless form. Rising took more effort than he cared to contemplate at that moment, but he clamped onto Kyle's hand and walked towards them to get a closer look. It was Tailor who lay prone on the floor, eyes glazed over in pain while the kid pressed down on a growing pool of blood seeping from the side of Tailor's gut.

"What happened?"

In a voice that shook with undisguised terror, the kid stammered out, "He t-tried to get that man off you." Lucas followed the flick of his gaze to Miles' body. "He was s-stabbed and I dragged him back here. Is he going to die?"

Lucas peeled the kid's hands back for a brief second to take a look at the wound then shared a solemn glance with Bastian. From the placement of the wound, it looked as though the knife had pierced Tailor's liver. There was no way to tell how much damage had been done. Even if they got him into surgery immediately, teleportation would only make it worse. The displacement could have harmful effects on exposed organs and tissue. It was why it was always necessary to close the eyes while travelling.

"I want to confess first. Please." Tailor's plea was hardly more than a whisper.

Bastian leaned in close. "I'd have to 'port you to the Queen. If I do that, your body will fail shortly afterwards."

A corner of Tailor's mouth quirked up in a faint grin. "Dying anyway. Please. I have to do this."

Bastian gathered the limp body in his arms as Lucas took the kid's hand in his free one. "Close your eyes, boy. We're going to the Queen's throne room."

A heartbeat after the kid obeyed, they appeared in the Queen's stately chamber and Lucas watched as Bastian laid Tailor on the floor in front of a surprisingly *un*surprised Queen. A Mackaeo member whom he knew to have the power of discerning the truth stood next to her and a small band of young humans stopped eating at a table to the side to stare at Bastian with avid interest.

He was missing something here but an explanation would have to wait until Tailor got out his last confession.

The young Tsielen told everything in short, broken sentences. Apparently, Connor had been enraged when Lucas had turned down his offer and left. Seeking a way to make up for the potential loss of the millions he would have made with Lucas' help, he'd turned to slavery. Tailor spoke of the abuse the weaker humans had endured under the harsh hands of Connor and his men before being sold to other Tsielen. It was at the end of his confession that his heart stopped beating and Bastian closed his eyes with his fingers.

The Queen looked to the member beside her who nodded once. Taking a fortifying breath, she addressed her guards in a clear voice. "Take this Tsielen away and give him a proper burial. He gave his life to adhere to the laws of his Queen and I will not have that sacrifice go unnoticed. I want a select group to begin an investigation into this apparent slave ring some of my people have chosen to participate in. As for you, Deluc, I'm assuming from your state of disarray that you took matters into your own hands and ended Connor's streak of tyranny?"

"I did, Your Majesty. After Bastian rescued my mate from him, I couldn't stand by and watch him restore his losses with more humans to sell. This boy," Lucas glanced to the cowering kid at his side, "would have become one of them."

Goosebumps rose over the kid's flesh and his hands flew to his groin as though he'd suddenly realised he stood in front of a crowd of people in only his underwear. Bastian jogged over, pulling the shirt from his back and tugging it onto the kid's smaller frame.

"I want to go home."

Lucas' heart constricted with shame and regret. He knew Connor would not have left the bedroom upstairs if the kid's parents had still been alive. "They're gone, little one. I didn't get there in time. I'm so sorry."

Instead of the tears, angry shouts or denials he had expected, the kid merely nodded his understanding. He was in shock. Sooner or later it would wear off and the kid would need a secure place to land on his feet. Lucas was more than willing to provide that but his life still hung on the verdict of his Queen. Looking to her, he patiently awaited whatever came next.

"Well, it seems that I have some serious decisions to make. You, Deluc, ran from your responsibility to the Mackaeo and subsequently to your race ten years ago. You killed the commander of my forces without my knowledge or consent. And you, Bastian, hid your power from your people and robbed them of the additional safety it would have brought them. You compromised the security of my home by bringing humans into it and failed to bring my commander in for questioning.

"All in all, I have to say...I'm impressed, despite the means you used to bring Connor's treachery to my attention. Most especially by this young man," she said, pointing a finger at Kyle. "I've never met a human willing to give his life and confront the Queen of an entire race to save the one he loves."

Lucas shot a disbelieving look at his mate, who had the audacity to smile shyly.

"It is an unorthodox mating but no less valid, I see. However, sentences for your crimes must be carried out. Therefore, I am charging Deluc and Bastian with the care of these seven humans..." She paused when Bastian cleared his throat.

"Uhh, that would be twelve in all...Your Highness. Five of the humans chose to stay at my cabin. I can assure you that they're still there. They understood the risk of Connor and his men finding them again without protection."

The Queen raised her brow at his interruption but continued when Bastian bowed his head in apology. "You will be responsible for *twelve* humans then, for the rest of their lives. I hereby exonerate you of the crimes you have committed against my laws under one circumstance." A small smile of anticipation played on her lips. "You will both make yourselves available for the teleportation of your Queen and her royal family to whichever destinations they choose, so long as it is with my permission or at my request."

Lucas blinked, waiting for the other shoe to drop. Bastian stared at him over the kid's head in equal confusion.

The Queen slapped her hands together and rubbed them in excitement. "I've always wanted my own personal teleporter. Now I have two. I'm giving you both one month to set up sufficient housing for yourselves and the humans using however much you need from the royal coffers. I'm planning a visit to Vienna soon that will be much more pleasant without the strain of travelling for hours on end. Oh, and gentlemen…"

Speechless, they could only stare at their Queen.

"Thank you for your services. It is appreciated more than you know."

Chapter Fourteen

Four weeks, one day and ten hours later

"Lucas! Luc, get your ass down here before I have to punish your mate myself!"

Lucas grinned at the frustration in his friend's tone. After all of his aliases, Kyle had put his foot down and demanded that everyone call him Lucas. Not that he minded. It was the name he'd had when his mate had first fallen in love with him. Speaking of which, he wasn't sure if he wanted to know what kind of trouble the little imp had got himself into this time.

After scrubbing the towel through his wet hair one more time, he tossed it into the hamper and quickly dressed. At about halfway down the stairs, he had to stop and take in the view of the people in his living room. Bastian held Kyle and Jules by the arms on either side of him while Amy stood back at a safe distance, trying unsuccessfully to hide a grin.

Both smaller men had bright red hair streaked with black framing pale faces. Their eyes were lined with kohl outliner that accentuated their colour. Sheer, black gauze moulded to their chests, allowing for tantalising glimpses of their nipples in the perfect lighting. Their tight, black leather pants rode low on their hips, topped off by heavy black boots with buckles and skulls. Lucas would be hard-pressed to find a more appealing sight.

"You gave them access to the internet again, didn't you?" Bastian accused.

Laughing, Lucas descended the rest of the stairs and came to stand in front of his mate. Eyeing the men up and down, he chuckled and sat down in his recliner. Kyle immediately ran to kneel on the floor between his legs, a look of repentant concern on his face. Running his fingers through his mate's hair, Lucas gloried in its silken texture.

"I gotta say, I think they look damn sexy."

"Did you not see what he did to my mate?" Bastian gestured to Jules, waving his hand to encompass the other man from head to toe.

"You're just worried that he'll be hit on by everything with two legs when you take him out tonight."

"Hell yeah I am! It's bad enough we can't keep our own hands off him. Amy and I won't be enough to fend off all the jealous assholes. I hold you responsible, so that means you two are coming with."

"Wait a minute," Lucas said, narrowing his eyes. "I'll bet anything that this was your mate's idea."

"And it was your mate that placed the order on your computer."

Glaring at each other, they turned to Amy. This wasn't the first time they'd butted heads over the trouble their mates got themselves into. As an interested third party,

Amy's opinion was usually used to settle differences, although at times Lucas wasn't always convinced of the objective stance she claimed she held. Her being mated to Bastian as well seemed to give his friend an advantage from Lucas' point of view.

Amy let out the laugh she'd been holding in then cleared her throat as they fixed her with an indignant stare. "Sorry. Okay, okay. In all fairness, both the little brats are to blame, and it would be nice to all go out together." She bounced over to Bastian and gave him a brief yet passionate kiss on the lips. "It's our first month anniversary and I won't let anything spoil it. Besides, I can't think of a better way to start off the day than by punishing our little mate."

Bastian growled down at her in mock irritation. "I think you're forgetting the difference between punishments and rewards."

Amy was coming into her own as a Dom and growing under Bastian's guidance, but she still had a long way to go towards learning patience.

"No she's not. Can we go? You can use that new toy you said you bought me." Jules bounced up and down, completely heedless of his Master's glower.

"If you'll excuse me," Bastian grumbled, "it seems I have a lesson to teach both of my mates. Nine o'clock. Don't be late. Wait, who's taking the Queen to Vienna tomorrow?"

"Rock, paper, scissors?"

Lucas shook his fist three times with Bastian and scowled when his scissors were crushed by the man's rock. His friend grinned triumphantly and left with his two mates in tow.

And the Queen had thought *his* mating was unconventional.

"So you're really not mad?"

"No baby, but you will be punished after my reward." At Kyle's confused look, he scooped up his mate and carried him through the kitchen and to a door which led to the basement. It was large, containing a ventilated gym, storage room and the dungeon he'd been working on since the construction crews had completed the renovations on the ranch style house he'd purchased using his Queen's money. Bastian's house, similar in size and style, had been built within close walking distance so that they could split the humans' living quarters between them yet remain nearby.

Setting his mate down, he opened the door and walked Kyle into their playroom. "I know we don't have the house to ourselves so I had this room soundproofed and locked with a key that only I have. The other pieces of furniture and toys should arrive here in the next week or so, but I thought we should break in what came yesterday."

Lucas gave Kyle a few moments to take it all in with his wide-eyed gaze. There wasn't enough yet to fill even half of the large room, but what was there was plenty to start out with. A spanking bench with several D-rings lining its sides was positioned against one wall with a suspension swing hanging from the ceiling beside it. Along the other side of the room stood a steel cage about three foot high by five and next to that was a display table with a glass top that lifted upward for easy access to the toys he had inside.

"Take off your clothes and fold them neatly on the chair behind you."

Kyle obeyed instantly, nearly tearing the thin fabric of his shirt in his haste. Lucas walked over to the table and picked out the toys he wanted. He could see his mate peeking out from the cover of his lashes in curiosity and suppressed his grin. He would reprimand him later for the slight, but for now he enjoyed the small victory of knowing Kyle's fear of pain was gone at last.

Leading Kyle over to the spanking bench, he directed him to fold his hands behind his back. Setting the toys aside, he kept one and held it out for his mate to see. "This is a cock and ball restraint. It will keep you from coming before I give you permission."

Kyle watched in fascination as Lucas took his semi-erect cock in hand and encased it in a series of six rings. His balls were pulled through the largest, separating them from his body, while the other five rings spanned the length of his cock. Each ring was smaller than the last with the smallest one fitting snugly just below the crown of his head.

Lucas turned his mate towards the bench and had him lean over it to grab the other side with his hands. Picking up the next toy, he squeezed a good amount of lube onto it then used his slicked fingers to stretch out Kyle's hole. His mate moaned and began bucking back. When Lucas felt he was ready, he withdrew his fingers and smacked the luscious ass sharply.

Kyle yelped, saying quickly, "Sorry, Sir."

"This is a prostate massager." He pushed the device in all the way so that the base rested against Kyle's cheeks. "I want you to hold it in until I take it out of you, is that understood?" He moved it up and down, pegging his mate's sweet spot before taking the remote control and turning it on to the lowest level. Kyle gave a startled gasp and tensed his muscles.

Taking the last toy in hand, a black suede whip, he rubbed his free hand over his mate's ass and back to give him warning. The first strike landed squarely across both cheeks and Kyle was forced to cling desperately to the bench. Lucas set a slow pace at first then gradually increased the strikes with each stronger setting of the massager. When Kyle's moans turned to cries, he eased the force of his lashes and brought the remote back down to the lowest setting.

A glance between his mate's legs revealed the straining of his cock against the rubber rings that prevented him from gaining a full erection. The harder Kyle became, the more pain he endured. Watching carefully and evaluating his mate's emotions for signs of stress, he went through the process again. The little man's chest heaved and a fine sheen of sweat coated his pale skin. Sinewy muscles writhed and bulged with the effort to hold himself in place without the benefit of cuffs strapping him down.

At the peak of the third cycle, he got the desired effect. Kyle threw his head back and screamed at the highest setting of the massager, tears rolling down his face unchecked. "Please, Master. Please may I come?"

Lucas's own cock strained against the confines of his pants at his mate's beautiful tears and pleas. Sucking in air to keep his raging arousal in check, he turned off the massager and slowed the speed of his strikes. When Kyle lay limp and panting, Lucas removed the toys gently and lifted his mate into the swing.

Cuffing Kyle's wrists on either side high above his head and his ankles to straps that opened his legs wide, bearing his glossy, puckered entrance, Lucas unbuckled his pants and freed his aching cock. Leaning forwards, he pulled

Kyle's head to his, plunging his tongue into his mouth and stealing his breath.

"I love it when you cry for me."

Lining up the head of his cock to Kyle's hole, he lunged forwards, driving his tongue in further at the same time to deny him the ability to cry out. His mate's tight channel gripped him fiercely until he couldn't hold back any longer. Straightening, he grasped Kyle's thighs firmly and pounded into him, using the sway of the swing and the punishing thrust of his hips to drive himself deeper and deeper. Lucas could feel Kyle's imminent climax in the mounting rush of pure joy that spread through their link.

"Master!"

"Now!" Lucas lost control as Kyle screamed again. His cock erupted, shooting jets of cum with each thrumming pulse, filling his mate completely. The orgasm seemed to last an eternity and it was all he could do to keep himself grounded as Kyle's love and pleasure bowled through him with overpowering ferocity.

When at last he was able to lean forwards without collapsing, he kissed his mate tenderly.

"You will always be mine."

The truth of that statement hit him with profound intensity. This was his forever, right here in the arms of the man who had challenged his worst fears to learn to love him. The man who had willingly faced death to rescue him from his enemy. Every day with him was a gift that he would treasure…forever.

About the Author

I have always been a lover of books, particularly those with the dichotomy of the strong alpha male and the weaker love of their life which they must rescue. After reading all I could find in M/F books, I decided to give M/M fiction a try and my addiction skyrocketed.

Hot, sexy men times two? No contest. Unfortunately, I was reading faster than the authors could produce. Eventually, I resorted to imagining my own stories and my mind took off from there.

I have to admit, though, I am a bit of a recluse. If not for the joy and humour my husband and four boys bring to me, I would never have ventured this far.

Nikki McCoy loves to hear from readers.

You can find her contact information, website details and author profile page at http://www.total-e-bound.com

Total-E-Bound Publishing

www.total-e-bound.com

Take a look at our exciting range of literagasmic™
erotic romance titles and discover pure quality
at Total-E-Bound.